T0367944

Tales
from the
Backyard

Tales
from the
Backyard

Stories told at dinner

CAROLYN GAYE

ARCHWAY
PUBLISHING

Archway Publishing books may be ordered through booksellers or by contacting:

Archway Publishing
1663 Liberty Drive
Bloomington, IN 47403
www.archwaypublishing.com
844-669-3957

Because of the dynamic nature of the Internet, any web addresses or links contained in this book may have changed since publication and may no longer be valid. The views expressed in this work are solely those of the author and do not necessarily reflect the views of the publisher, and the publisher hereby disclaims any responsibility for them.

Any people depicted in stock imagery provided by Getty Images are models, and such images are being used for illustrative purposes only. Certain stock imagery © Getty Images.

ISBN: 978-1-6657-6424-7 (sc)
ISBN: 978-1-6657-6425-4 (e)

Library of Congress Control Number: 2024916077

Print information available on the last page.

Archway Publishing rev. date: 11/07/2024

"Memories are like a good souffle; better when lingered over and preferably shared."

Contents

DESSERT AND BRANDY

Introduction

To share your stories is a human impulse. To be heard validates your existence, especially if you have passed the midlife mark and events from long ago begin receding into the mist.

Imagine being in your later years when those around you are distracted after a few minutes if you start talking about the good old days. Then, suddenly, you are invited to dinner and are surprised to find you have the host's undivided attention. Your host lets you ramble on until thoughts and foggy recollections begin to rearrange themselves and coalesce into a logical, easy to remember story. Almost magically, you have something to hang your hat on. Instead of disjointed images and fragments of memories that didn't add up to much, you now have a coherent tale that enriches your life history. Even if the story happened to someone else, it enlivens your world view and there is probably a reason that it personally rang true and inspired you to tell the tale.

Pretend, if you will, that the host invited other individuals to share an evening and a story. Just like the people who tell them, some of the sharings are brief, to the point, and have been wrapped up before the appetizers are gone. Others revel in the attention, but the point is made before dessert, and a few are long winded and go on into the night with the aid of a brandy or two.

A song from the Broadway musical *Rent* asks, how do you measure a lifetime? It tells us there are 525,600 minutes in a year; how can we shape our experiences so that they add up to something memorable and not just a string of events? Scientists say our brain can take in a quadrillion pieces of information in a lifetime, but we forget 50% of what we learn within an hour. Given this overwhelming amount of information our minds confront, how *can* we measure a lifetime.

Stories are a way to accomplish this; they connect the dots—bits of half-forgotten moments—and bring them back to life. They activate and synthesize multiple parts of our brain, including emotions and senses, so we are more likely to hold onto those minutes of life that can be shared with others in a way they might find compelling.

When we take stock of our lives it becomes clear that we only have memories as a yardstick. We surround ourselves with photographs and favorite things that provide touchstones to help jog these memories loose, 'Oh, yes, I remember that day, that house, those people and pets', but mostly, we are left with floating images and thoughts that are hard to grasp unless we have arranged this jigsaw of memory into a narrative pattern—a story. What better way to crystallize these life experiences than to share them at dinner.

APPETIZERS

Red Shoes

When I was young, my shoes were made for the city. Sleek, red and pretty, but they were strong, and they made me feel I could do anything. Let's go shoes, I'd say, and we would walk 20 blocks on hot pavement; bound over tree roots that pushed the sidewalk up just as you were passing by; dodge oncoming crowds pressing forward as though you were invisible.

Suddenly, I saw you and you saw me. Time collapsed—the indifferent crowd pushed us along and we went our separate ways.I thought of you later, standing in the vast field that I had escaped. I clicked my red shoes and smiled.

Greyhound Bus

Back in the day, many people left home and family on a Greyhound. In 1965, it was my turn. I was first in line at the depot, fidgeting with my ticket and shifting from foot to foot. Ready for my future in the city, I waited there with my tan suitcase and my new pierced earrings.

The bus to San Francisco pulled up and after a long minute the driver opened the door with a click and a swish. He appeared on the steps, leaned out and called 'All Aboard'! That first step up felt like Mt Everest and took determination to scale it; I was leaving everything behind.

I settled into a window seat as others boarded. A three-or four-year-old sitting across the aisle caught my eye and smiled conspiratorially; she knew we were both off on an adventure. I smiled and nodded. It was getting dark as Sacramento faded away—I turned on my reading light and began an article about a new book by Betty Friedan, 'The Feminine Mystique'. I mused on the article while watching the driver's silhouette against the windshield—we were barreling into the future.

Snapshot 1968

I know you don't believe me—that we had dogs and cigarettes in college classrooms back then. Here's proof in my shoebox of old photos. This picture is of a psychology class in Berkeley. The People's Park demonstration is happening outside the window and there are mounted police milling through the crowd.

Everyone's wearing headbands and boots. See, there's a German Shepard and a black Labrador lounging in the aisles; I can still hear their ting-a-ling collars and sighs of comfort. The window highlights plumes of cigarette smoke while the goateed professor is at the front of the classroom earnestly discussing a long-ago problem with an attractive young lady.

It must be a Monday because we are all playing chess. We devoted the start of each week to this game—the teacher swore by it as a way to learn assertiveness and other psycho-social skills. He said it was a microcosm of human psychology and interaction—fortunately, this is not necessarily true because I usually lost.

I Could Walk to Work

The fog often breaks at Columbus Avenue and leaves North Beach's Telegraph Hill basking in the sun. People would say 'best weather in the city, besides the Mission District'. Mornings like that made you want to set the alarm clock early to experience its freshness. Rolling down the hill from your place, it was easy to tell where the old Italians lived—their blinds were closed to avoid fading the furniture. Newer arrivals to North Beach—office workers, hippies, leftover Beats, they usually pulled their blinds high and often sat by the window or even on the sill. Taking your clothes to the laundromat could be a pleasure on mornings like that.

On the way to the Financial District there was often time to stop at Café Trieste for a 'duo cappuccino' and to check out the paper—then continue a block or two out of your way, through Chinatown, and you would enter another world. Sidewalks glistened wet after vegetable stall vendors hosed them down, and you could count on a rooster or two crowing from the rooftops.

Set 'Em Up Joe

One rainy night, not long after Priscilla flew off to southern California, her two ex-husbands were surprised to find themselves sitting on neighboring stools in a gritty mid-town bar. It was a slow night and after they had bought each other several whiskeys they began entertaining the bartender with stories about the woman who drove them to drink.

The juke box was playing Sinatra's 'Set Em Up Joe', and Priscilla's most recent husband sang a few words along with Sinatra, 'I got a story you ought to know'. He said, "she's going to learn the meaning of money now—nothing gets you up close and personal with reality than poverty."

"Tell me about it," chimed in both the first husband and bartender.

"She'll barely get by on the alimony I can give her, but she's spending it in advance," continued the second husband.

The first husband said, "Sounds familiar. When you've got money for trips, fine dining and the like, you can call each other *Honey* and *Dear* more easily."

At this, the bartender poured three more drinks on the house and toasted Priscilla, "May the good lady be a miser with her money or find a rich old man."

The three clinked glasses and sank into a quiet moment.

Paint for Brains

I no longer carry my paintbox everywhere—no need when I've got a complete set in my brain, an infinite assortment of colors, blends and washes. Eyeballs are my paintbrush, they sweep back and forth across the canvas, stopping here and there for details. They know how to apply just the right amount of paint and how to add highlights to perfection. Color mixing is a snap.

Look at that morning sky! Let's see, lots of Cerulean Blue with a very light turquoise glaze blending into peach and a touch of Lemon Yellow setting off Camelback Mountain (Burnt Umber and Sienna with touches of reflected sky color).

Survey the mental image, remove some of the Lemon Yellow, add Marine Blue glaze to top of sky, finish with a gloss glaze to the whole thing. Done in two minutes, hands are clean and no need for more supplies. Can't sell these paintings, but they are always perfect.

MAIN COURSE

Lady of Spain

Helen Vandevere, the celebrated ornithologist, no longer trekked mountains and streams to witness the antics of birds, but her memories remained as vivid as if she was sitting on a riverbank watching birds hopping from tree to tree. Now, behind closed eyes she could rewind her adventures of those colorful days.

How the freedom of her adult life contrasted with her stultifying early years as an only child, living in the tiniest of houses with parents who put too much stock in her. She wondered what they would do with themselves if she wasn't there for them to curate her every move.

Breakfast, lunch and dinner, she was squeezed between them at a small table that was crammed into a kitchen corner. It was alright when she was little, but as she grew bigger, it was suffocating. Her mother was a housewife whose life's purpose was to care for this tiny house, a blustery but insecure husband, and Helen.

Her father was a Union representative for the railroad and saw himself as a pillar of the small town, and his self-importance was wrapped up in the admiration he felt was his due in the Union hierarchy. Helen thought he didn't see her, only his image of her as a perfect child, a well-behaved emissary that represented him to the town. 'Remember, people notice how you conduct yourself, your father is an important man in the Union and people need to have confidence in him. How can they have confidence in him if his only child misbehaves?' Nothing could be worse.

Helen's little house was isolated near a wetland on a major bird migration flyway in the San Joaquin Valley. She was not allowed to roam freely, so often she had to be satisfied with watching the feathered procession from her front porch each spring and fall as thousands of geese, ducks, sandpipers and others landed in the wetland or flew overhead on their way to Tule Lake. It was natural for her to identify with their freedom; they weren't hemmed in at a breakfast nook. Helen wanted to know more about their behavior, but she wasn't satisfied with the scientist's explanation that they navigate by the electromagnetic field and the stars, end of discussion. That didn't explain everything, there was so much more to learn about the birds, earth and stars.

Her father loved the sound of the accordion, and it was his dearest wish that Helen make him proud by learning to play it. When she was 13, an unlucky number, he announced that she would play a piece at the Union meeting in a few days. She tried to beg off, explaining that if she did it the following year, she would be able to play it perfectly, but not next week.

As usual, her plea for understanding fell on closed ears. Just imagining all those expectant faces staring up at her made her legs go rubbery, and as the evening grew closer, she yearned to fly away.

The night of the meeting, she watched the room fill up with people looking expectantly at her as she stood there in her Sunday dress, clutching the accordion in front of her as if in self-protection from the crowd. When she found her parents' smiling faces floating up from the middle chairs, she thought she noted a touch of apprehension flickering across her mother's face.

Her damp hands shook as she squeezed out the first few notes of *Lady of Spain*. They sounded alright, so she plowed ahead, *Lady of Spain I adore you, Lady of Spain, I implore you...* but soon realized she couldn't remember how the rest of the damn thing went, so she went on into musical oblivion and couldn't stop playing *Lady of Spain, I adore you, Lady of Spain, I implore you...*over and over and over. Helen saw her mother looking at her knees, her father's beet-red face, and she heard the beat of wings.

The Little Old Man

The little old couple lived by the sea. They were devoted to each other—at least she was devoted to him, and he was quite happy with the arrangement. She knit them identical sweaters, so it was hard to tell them from apart from a distance. She made everything perfect for him and anticipated his every need. Eagle-eyed on their seaside walks, she removed any obstacles in his path lest he might trip. He could rest assured that if the wind took a nippy turn on the boardwalk, she would pull a wool scarf from her handbag to keep him cozy, and she always had his favorite snacks should he desire something to nibble. In winter, they timed their walks to match the sunset and if the sun made a particularly brilliant performance, he would applaud, grab her by the waist, and spin her around in a few dance steps.

One day the little old lady didn't wake up and for a long time, the grey sky covered the setting sun. The little old lady's little old sister had no patience for her brother-in-law and thought her sister a fool to spend so much of herself on a man who never lifted a finger for her. But after a while, she began feeling guilty doing nothing for him, so she invited him to a big party with lots of blue-haired ladies who were delighted to see him. He did ask one frowsy woman to dance and told her he was attracted to the splashy, orange dress she wore—it reminded him of the setting sun, but when the music stopped, he thanked her and took a cab home.

The thought of her brother-in-law alone every day and night preyed on her mind, and she brought over a stray dog her neighbor had rescued.

"Here," she said, handing over the little mutt. "I think you both could use a companion." But the dog never looked at the man or listened to his commands, and it treated the man like the dog was in charge. The sister-in-law watched how the dog ruled the house and thought 'I'll be, how unexpected'.

She still couldn't see what had attracted her sister to this man with a pudgy belly, hair in all the wrong places, and his habit to take, take, take. What was her sister thinking? So, she ignored him, except on Sundays when she'd bring over a pie. She felt sorry to see him sitting Sunday after Sunday on the couch with the dog, and eventually she brought him a stew and then a casserole, "Only because I made too much."

Then one weekday she popped over with freshly baked loaves of bread.

"I made too many," she explained.

He had been on his way out and was closing the door when she arrived.

"Thanks."

"Let me just put these on a high shelf," she said, "away from the dog."

"I'm going for a walk on the beach. You can come along if you want."

She couldn't believe it when she heard herself say, "Oh yes, please."

"Is that a new hat?"

"Oh, no, this old thing?"

"Have you got a snack?"

Man of My Dreams

Fred and I had always dreamed of a trip to Venice and now there we were, spending a night in a 17th century Pallazo on the Grand Canal. A dream come true, but humidity that arose from the canal made my sleep fitful and I worried that without enough rest I wouldn't feel up for the next day.

It looked like Fred was having a hard time sleeping as well. He was snoring softly when he wasn't kicking at the expensive silky sheets and every now and then he'd turn in a way that told me the soft feather bed was hurting his back. I could empathize, my neck hurt, and I longed for my pillow back home.

I turned on the TV and found the end of a Marcello Mastrianni movie—what a man. Marcello had charming good looks, humor, gravitas, and that glorious head of hair, all in one package. Marcello's lovely voice lulled me into a floating world.

I slipped in and out of dreamland where Marcello waited for me. The sound of Fred's snoring became a motorboat and when he turned to ease his back the old mattress lifted me like a wave. Then Marcello was my gondolier with a red neck-scarf and striped tee-shirt. He sang to me as we glided through a golden transcendent city.

Thunder and lightning crashed outside the Pallazo window and interrupted the idyl. I had read about violent storms that arose without warning on the Adriatic and sank countless ancient mariners. On the sidewalk I heard young people's laughter as they ran for shelter.

The rain cooled the night air and soon I closed my eyes again, but now I was clinging to the gondola, and we were out past the lagoon in the middle of a stormy sea. Marcello was at the helm, his red neck scarf and striped tee-shirt rippling in the wind, but they were strangely dry. The little boat creaked and bobbed wildly as Marcello turned to me with his Marcello smile and again my heart was his.

"Do not be afraid, Bella Mia," he shouted over the thunder, "the storm will pass, and I am the best gondolier in all of Venice." This would have been more reassuring had I not remembered that my pilot had been dead for quite a while.

My eyes popped open to a fresh gauzy-yellow Venetian light streaming in the room. A seagull squawked past the window and a bottle of spicy Campari glowed ruby-red in front of the mirror. Fred was awake, and as usual, studying the ceiling.

I would always ask, "What in the world are you thinking?" He would always answer "Oh, just cogitating."

That became our joke, whenever one of us were possibly wasting time, we would dignify dreaminess with 'oh, just cogitating'.

I struggled to upright myself on the soft mattress. The lovely sheets were in a heap on the floor.

I yawned and said, "How was your night?" It always felt like the darkness separated us into distant universes and mornings were a time to reconnoiter. "You were pretty restless."

"You too," he said, as he pulled a pillow feather out of my tangled hair, "this bed belongs in a museum. I had the funniest dream I was a gondolier."

Downstream

Jeb, a heavily bearded mountain man, poked his canoe into the reeds and his skillful use of the paddle let him turn with agility. He made beaver noises and called 'chucachuca—cachuchuca', then listened for a slap or rustle.

He had seen trappers setting up camp the other day—they were a rough looking bunch, and he knew his limitations now that he was old. He warned them to stay away from his pond by sounding a buffalo horn three times a day, a tradition laying claim to the area. He had turned his back on society long ago and retreated to the mountains where he could ruminate, and now he barely remembered what the final straw was that made him hightail it off to the woods and leave the world behind. It wasn't one thing—he had often escaped to the mountains when it was all too much for him in town, and returned when he felt better, but then one time he just stayed. He didn't regret it, but his anger had dissipated, and he grew lonely over the years. It was harder to get around now; his dog had died long ago and the young beaver he had nursed to health became his companion.

Seeing the trappers preparing to turn his friend into a beaver hat brought back the anger he felt when he was living in town—people were selfish, uncaring brutes and their arrival at the pond brought back his discontent with the world. Jeb admired beavers, they only built things, they didn't destroy. They chewed down some trees, but that didn't hurt the big woods; the ponds added to the water table and gave sustenance to wildlife. Every day now he went looking for traps and undid them—he wanted to destroy them, but he was afraid of the brutes who might come and take revenge. His fighting days were over.

The older beavers that built the dam had moved downstream, but the young bachelor beaver remained in the upper pond because he'd had a skirmish with a fox and his tail got in the way. Jeb patched up the beaver while calming it in his low, soothing voice, and for the next year he watched as 'Buddy' recuperated and started improving the dam.

After a few days of searching, Jeb paddled downstream and, just as he hoped, there was his beaver-friend, slapping the water with his tail like there was nothing wrong with it, energetically stacking twigs and branches to build a new dam with his equally busy mate. Jeb had been alone too long, burdened with too many emotions, and they flooded him all at once with both relief at finding the little beaver family alive and busy, and with sadness at his personal loss of a daily connection to another living being. There was also fear that he could not protect the new family so far downstream.

Emotions continued to plague him on his arduous trip back up the river; he built a fire when he finally arrived at the upper pond and broodily stared into the flames. Jeb upbraided himself for not building a better house—he had lost track of how long it had been since he built the rough little cabin that was supposed to be temporary. Was he stalling to build a better house because that would mean he'd never get back to town?

He hadn't built a suitable cabin even though he almost

froze to death the last winter as the north wind blew the chinks out of the cracks in the walls and whistled through the room. He patched up the holes that he could reach, but even this simple task proved too strenuous and he saw that decrepitude was around the corner—how could he build an entire new cabin now?

Jeb admired the industry of the beavers along the river. In the same period of time he had been languishing in that cold cabin, they had constructed so much—every day chewing down small trees, pulling off branches, hauling and stacking the wood to create a cozy home and productive pond. But what else had they to do?

He ruminated on this and poked irritably at the fire. They don't worry about society trapping them, they don't waste time discussing things to no end, and they don't expect too much so they aren't disappointed when things don't work out.

The next day he was so distracted with plans to keep the beavers safe he stepped squarely into a hidden trap. The pain was as excruciating as he often thought it would be for the unfortunate beavers or other animals caught by its iron claw. Screaming in pain he tried to release its hold on his ankle, but he found he could not get a good angle on it and lay there waiting to die, either by the loss of blood or at the hands of an angry, no-good trapper. He knew the bone was broken, why did they make it so strong for a little beaver, and fury overcame his pain.

His thoughts jumbled together, anger and pain gave way to blankness, but he snapped to attention when he heard a sound in the brush. In his confusion, for an instant he thought it was the beaver returning to rescue him, but quickly adrenaline cleared his head. Images of a mountain lion or wolf lurking out there, or a vulture waiting patiently in the tall grasses for his demise filled his imagination. This made him cry, not from the pain or fear, but because he was sorry he had not led a more productive life.

"So, there you are, you old trap-steeling rascal, live by the sword, die by the sword, eh? What am I supposed to do with you?"

Another man said, "He deserves what he got, you're too soft, besides, what can we do out here in the wilderness?

Jeb was too weak to reply, by now he was drained of anger and fear—only a tiny emotion was left at the bottom of his soul, and he recognized it as a flicker of hope. In the cabin at night he had passed the time by reading, the same books over and over, so he had memorized them and an Emily Dickinson poem came to mind, *Hope is a Thing with Feathers*.

Other than this poem, all earthly thoughts, even his overweening pride, receded from consciousness. All he could hoarsely say was a barely audible "please."

The rest was a blur as the trappers undid the mechanical jaw and somehow dragged him onto a horse. The next thing he knew, he smelled whiskey on a man leaning over him, someone he heard referred to as 'Doc'.

"Can you hear me? You can thank these trappers for bringing you here to Virginia City, another few hours in the sun and you'd have had it, for sure."

The friendlier trapper took a bottle of whiskey out of Doc's hand and passed it to Jeb.

He said, "Drink this, old-timer, you'll need it for the amputation."

The best that could be said about the operation was that it was over quickly, and he was too weak to scream loudly.

With only one foot, an old man couldn't make it upstream and live in the wilds. He stayed in Virginia City helping Doc put people back together. He liked to think his own sober ways helped the Doc cut down on the whiskey, but he understood the Doc's job could lead a person to drink, what with the ghastly mining accidents and wildlife encounters that came in. One man shot at a bear and only made it angry—somehow Doc made a patchwork out of the torn parts and managed to get his scalp sewn back on pretty much in one piece.

Jeb was impressed with Doc and found that these days he had little complaint with the society of people downstream in Virginia City—it was only a few individuals that let you down, but he tried not to dwell on that. He couldn't make the trip back to the pond, but he took Miss Dickenson's poem to heart about hope having feathers and he hoped hard for the little family busily tending to their pond since Doc told him that beaver hats were going out of style.

The Wizards of Oz

It wasn't my idea to snoop on Uncle Gregory, but I needed the general science class anyway and my grandmother was always good at bribing me. She was worried that her baby brother was having a breakdown from all the science he read. "It's all so confusing, it can muddle your brain, I can't tell whether he's talking gibberish or it's science".

I walked into class late, and Uncle Gregory looked a little more wild-eyed than usual. He was in mid-lecture, his arthritic back bent over so far he had to strain his neck to challenge the students straight in the eye.

"I ask you young whippersnappers, do we get wiser as we get older?"

The students knew a trap when they heard one and this professor was known for marking you down if you argued with him.

He croaked, "Do we? Do We? Okay, I'll tell you."

The class looked relieved and there was a collective sigh.

We won't get wiser if we don't have the information that we need to think. Algorithms are spoon feeding information, little stingy pipelines of information that don't give us enough to work with to get new ideas and creative solutions. They give us tunnel vision, as if you're looking through a telescope clearly at a little island, but you are missing the big ocean. This flattens our knowledge base."

The class looked confused. He wrote on the old-school blackboard that was specially ordered for him and pieces of chalk flew everywhere.

> *Information is Power!*
> *If the machine does our thinking for us, who do*
> *you think will run the world? We are being spoon-*
> *fed pieces of information!*

There was a murmur of recognition in the class, comments could be heard, like 'that's not good', and 'but it's out of our hands'.

"Your homework last week was to see The Wizard of Oz. The people of Oz were being controlled by a puny guy behind a big curtain and a big voice—he was able to pull the strings that controlled their lives because he had all the information, even though he was a wimp.

In tomorrow's Oz, if you pull back the curtain you will see big computers with puny programmer wizards typing algorithms. Is that what you want?"

"No way!" Said the class, visibly concerned.

"Good!" Said Uncle Gregory. He got new chalk and wrote,

> *Progress—for you or the wizards?!*

"Okay, whippersnappers, only you can prevent tyranny of the machine!"

With that he hummed the Looney Tunes theme and in one last flurry of chalk particles, he wrote on the board and hobbled out of the room, never to return.

That's All Folks!

The class looked confused. Is class over? 'That's one weird dude,' and 'talk about the nutty professor'.

When my grandmother grilled me about her baby brother, I was noncommittal. I didn't want to upset her by saying he had gone around the bend, or worse, that he might be right.

Elevator Operator

I admit it, I am uniform-proud. Mine is pert blue with gold buttons and topped off with a smart-looking pillbox hat; the ensemble makes me feel like a stewardess. I know who I am in my uniform and people treat me with respect, even if they keep their distance—I think they understand not to be familiar with someone who might have their life in their hands. I may be overdramatizing here, it's not like I'm really a stewardess or in the military. But see, my overactive imagination is the result of constant chattering to myself —I have so much time to think, and my internal monologue goes on all day. My mind flits from one thing to the next in seconds and I can have a few thoughts in between the first and second floor.

Up and down, up and down. Surprises are few in the life of an elevator operator, and I've learned to entertain myself with the slightest event in my little kingdom and then embroider it with many variations throughout the day. Did I say, 'my little kingdom'? Yes, there I go again, I've been told that I self-aggrandize at times—one minute I'm a stewardess flying the airplane due to some emergency in the cockpit, the next minute I'm queen of my square little kingdom, but what's the alternative? Would it be better to look at unadorned reality straight in the eye, so to speak, and after 20 years of taking this crate up 18 floors and back down again, should I feel like a gerbil, forever treading and getting nowhere?

Some days I'm clear-eyed and reality centric. These are not my better days. I am more sensitive to the motions inherent in elevators—the nausea that comes with the elevator's lurch at every floor. My doctor says that it's butterflies and probably due to anxiety, perhaps fear of heights. Am I anxious? I don't know, I avoid thinking about how high up we are at the top of the building by filling my mind with nonsensical chatter for the rest of the ride. Like I said, some days are better than others and I feel better when I think that stewardesses must have the same feeling at takeoff.

It is company policy not to be familiar with the passengers and to keep my social distance. I think so much that my mind is overflowing with ideas and impressions, but I can't offload them like I do people at their floors. If I overhear a conversation, I'm stuck with unresolved questions that were cut off with the closing of the elevator doors. Or I see headlines at lunch, and there is no one to ask about these things, even though I'm the stewardess and queen of all I survey. I am in awe of these people who go off down the hallways to enter closed doors and succeed at mysterious jobs that I probably would not know where to start.

In truth, I'm not sure if my passengers are merely abiding with company policy to not be familiar with me or are they a little standoffish. Do they just see me as a fixture of the elevator. I know that my diffidence doesn't help. Hard to break through that wall to communication and embark on a discussion about who I think will win the Kentucky Derby or what are the chances for world peace. I have a few friends outside of the building, but we always go drinking at Paoli's and after awhile they are not really listening, they're stuck on their own inner monologue.

Not only am I uniform-proud, I am also floor-status proud. I am not a snobby person, honestly, but this is a result of equating each floor with the importance of my passengers' jobs and the quality of their uniforms, or rather, clothes. You can't let people off on these floors without noticing that above the 16th floor there is a plushily carpeted hall, philodendrons on marble tables that set off polished walnut paneling, and that the lack of street noise creates a rich-sounding silence. It's a rarified atmosphere for the higher-ups, and the closer you get to the 18th floor the more important you are. This is what I like about my job, I get to 'mingle' with people from the higher echelons, if only for a minute. I am outside that rigid social status.

The other day, a group of hippies got on at the lobby and rode up to the 16th floor. Apparently, they knew a somewhat important person on that floor. I couldn't stop myself from peeking at them from the level of my stool, I hoped they didn't notice. They seemed free; the girls had easy laughs, long flowing hair, and gauzy dresses. The rest of the day I was uncomfortable—my pill box hat felt heavy, and I pushed it so far back on my head it almost fell off.

Most days my job is okay. It's company policy to be cheerful and I am a cheerful person by nature, so that is not a problem, but I'm beginning to bristle at the policy not to fraternize. According to policy, a pleasant good morning, a friendly comment on the weather or an upcoming holiday was fine, but then that wall comes down. However, I shouldn't complain, I still like the rhythms of the day. The morning rush exhilarates me, there is usually an energy in the car that I can vicariously absorb. Except for the sleepyheads, most everyone has an agenda, and I overhear many of them talk about their meetings and tasks for the day. My plan for the next eight hours is to go up and down and offer hundreds of polite helloes, but I'm used to that.

The same thing happens in reverse as people leave for the evening or weekend. Despite my 'royal status' and my ability to take over the controls of an airplane for an emergency landing, I'm becoming more sensitive to the monotony in my life. I can feel the inertia settling in and probably will do nothing about it— I've gone through this before and believe this uneasiness will pass.

One day, the mail room supervisor from the 2nd floor said, "You know, Margaret, I can tell if you are having an up day or a down day by the way you wear your hat. Today, you have it at a jaunty angle, so you must be feeling pretty good. Last week, it was pushed to the back of your head, so I figured you were tired."

"Pardon me"?

I couldn't believe my ears; this was a very personal thing to say. I knew his name because Mike was embroidered in red on his beige mailroom smock. The elevator had always been full when he arrived at 7:45 am and left at 5:00 pm, and he was rarely standing close enough in the elevator to address me. I didn't think he knew my name, but then I remembered it was written in big, looping, gold letters on my pin. It pleased me to have him take notice of my hat, or by extension, my uniform, but I didn't know how to respond.

Should I be pleased at the attention of a nice-looking man or affronted at his familiarity. Surely, even people on the 2nd floor understand the code of the uniform. I decided to 'go with the flow' as I heard the hippies in the elevator say. I liked that expression, to go with the flow, wherever the breeze takes you, consequences be damned.

All that went through my mind by the time we went up one floor and Mike stepped out into the noisy tiled, uncarpeted foyer. Mail carts that looked and sounded like clanking shopping carts were competing with street noise, nothing like the atmosphere for the higher-ups. I hadn't answered, and he was about to disappear down the hall into the distinctly unmysterious mailroom.

"What about when it's squarely on top of my head?"

He stopped, turned around, and pinned me with those interesting eyes. "I don't know, you tell me."

I was speechless and forgot to close the elevator door even though someone on the executive's 18th floor was ringing for me.

He laughed and said, "Have a good day, Margaret."

On the way up to the executive floor, I thought about what uniform my passenger would be wearing. Probably a silk tie and a Hong Kong-tailored suit of fine weave. The men on the middle floors, like the Purchasing Dept on the 9th floor often had clip-on ties and boring department store suits that didn't always fit them well across the shoulders. I excused myself for being both a uniform and floor snob, it came with the territory.

Like I mentioned, I can have a thought or two per floor and on the way up to the 18th floor I also thought about Mike. He was rather handsome with dark hair and eyes that looked into you. However, the burlap-colored smock with Mike written in red is not a good uniform and he works on the 2nd floor.

Deal breaker, I thought.

Even I am surprised at the rapidity at which these thoughts zip in and out of my mind. I could make an important decision between floors.

A dignified looking, silver-haired man in a gorgeous windowpane suit stepped in and said, "2nd floor, please."

I heard myself say out loud in an unusually high voice, "The mail room, sir?"

"I have to tell Mike I'll be a few minutes late for our tee-time."

The chattering voice in my head went dumb, and apparently, I forgot how to drive the elevator. The light on the 14th floor came on and I turned the lever to stop but overshot the landing by a foot and had to do some serious jockeying to get back to level. I could see from the corner of my eye the executive lurching back and forth with these maneuvers.

Mortified, I said in a small voice, "I'm very sorry, sir." I glanced at him, but he didn't seem to mind, in fact he was suppressing a laugh.

"I've ridden with or you for years and you've always been so perfect. It's good to see you can make a mistake."

All I managed was a snorting kind of giggle. Oh, no, that didn't sound like a stewardess' laugh, where did that unsophisticated sound come from, why are all my words stuck in my head?

The 7th floor light went on and I turned the lever more carefully to prevent a repetition of the 14th floor incident. I only hoped that the executive didn't tell Mike about that silly elevator operator who snorts when she giggles.

Teri the Terodactyl

Back when we were still able to walk 5 miles without requiring medical attention, we camped at the far end of Lake Chabot in the hills that divided the San Francisco Bay and Contra Costa Valley.

It was hard to sleep with all the noise—the hooting owls, singing frogs, splashing fish, and the breeze off the Bay rustling through the pines and eucalyptus. We didn't want to close our eyes though, not only to keep a lookout for imagined mountain lions, but to peek through the swaying treetops at Orion's Belt and Cassiopia's knee. It was all an unexpected beauty a few miles above the freeways.

The next morning, we left our woodland friends, flagged down the little Lake Chabot ferry and settled into our seats. We were enjoying the pristine morning when a nerve-jangling helicopter appeared out of nowhere and headed to the highest part of the eastern hill that overlooked both the lake on one side and the Contra Costa Valley on the other. The sound chopped through the quiet morning and Jim said, "great, now civilization has found us, what are they doing, looking for criminals in that forest?

The helicopter hovered over the highest trees for what seemed like an age—what was it going to do? The wait piqued our curiosity and we made guesses about what would happen next; nothing prepared us to see big, green bushy things about the size of Christmas trees being scattered onto the treetops. "No, wait, those can't be what I think they are," said Jim, they look like Christmas trees." A check with the driver of the ferry confirmed that the Parks Department was recycling those trees—they were perfect for great blue heron roosts. We would never have guessed that.

Years later, our family moved into a tract house in Contra Costa Valley that came complete with a koi pond built by the previous owner. Stargazing and birdwatching had been pushed aside by midlife responsibilities and the closest thing we had to nature in our daily lives was the koi pond.

Watching the koi became our way to unwind—we put comfortable chairs by the pond and the children slowly fed them. We would sit with a glass of wine and made a game of trying to count them and over the years we always came up with different numbers—they were continually moving and when they turned, their red, white, and black markings morphed like kaleidoscopes into different shapes as they moved. We agreed there were either 16 or 17 and left it at that. Some had more personalities than others—Beggar, Bully, Speed-freak and Acrobat—that's how we were able to keep track of at least some of them.

There was something else watching our koi. One morning I sensed a shadow passing overhead in our suburban sky. I looked up and there, high above, was a huge bird slowly flapping its 6' wings and circling the neighborhood. Immediately I thought of the Lake Chabot rookery and how, from that height, the herons could see the valley from their ariel vantage. I looked at the huge bird that was looking for breakfast and then at the pond where the koi were patiently waiting for their Koi Chow. Then I saw the black netting covering the apricot tree to fend off little birds who loved our apricots. It would be a shame to lose those apricots, but there was triage to be done. Besides, the little birds had to eat too. I managed to pull the net off the tree and when the netting was over the pond and the two-million-year-old bird out of sight, I went about my more normal morning routine.

Our kindergartner was home with a fever and napping on a couch that faced the backyard. Janie had probably gotten the fever from her older sister, whose temperature had dramatically risen so high it made her hallucinate hamburgers. After an ice bath didn't bring her temperature down, we all piled in the car and headed to the hospital. Janie was scared when she saw her sister brushing the bedcovers and saying, 'get these hamburgers off my bed' and now she was worried she'd get an ice bath and see hamburgers too.

When Janie opened her eyes, the first thing she saw was a 4' tall bluish bird that looked like the picture of a Pterodactyl on the wall in her classroom. This creature was staring directly at her, or more likely, at its reflection in the floor to ceiling patio window. It was hard for her to believe it was not a hallucination and she wanted to go to the hospital too and skip the ice bath. She was inconsolable until she realized it would make a good story. She told everyone about the bird she hallucinated that was big as a man and made it official by naming it Teri Terodactyl.

We moved soon after and donated the fish to the Oakland Museum for their pond that held 300 koi. Bully, Beggar, Speed-freak, Acrobat and the rest of them would be safer there, surrounded by city buildings, and if Teri Terodactyl did venture down 10th Street, it would only be an unlucky one to get caught out of 300 fish. The curator's assistant came from the Museum with an oxygenated trailer, and it took hours to corral them. In all the years we watched these placid fish swim lazily in circles, we never imagined them flying far out of the water and transforming into turbojets when confronted.

Acrobat even leapt 10 feet out of the pond to where I was standing. I tried to make an impossible catch before he hit the cement, but at least I broke his fall, and he survived. The struggle that afternoon reminded me of my karate teacher from years before who said, "Be like carp (koi), they fight to the end, but when they know it's over, they lie still and prepare for the end."

We often visited the Museum café that overlooked the koi pond. We never tried to count them, but we could pick out Beggar and Acrobat because of their obvious personalities. I wished them luck—although we were in the heart of the city, Lake Chabot was only a few miles away.

Sunday Dinners

It was my 12th birthday that New Year's weekend in 1956 when my parents tried to sneak me past a casino side lounge in Reno. I shook my arm loose from my mother's firm hold to glimpse an entertainer wearing the fanciest shirt I'd ever seen. He was brimming with confidence and gusto while crooning into a handheld microphone; the audience was mesmerized. I wanted to be that performer—I wanted people to listen to me like that and to not have parents dragging me around all the time.

My mother regained possession of my arm and said, "Tony, stop dawdling, we'll be late for the floor show."

The vision of future Tony slipped away for the time being and we were off to see an old lady in a lavender gown reminiscing on end about songs I'd never heard before. Years later, the image of being the center of attention that the lounge singer represented stayed with me. When I peeked through that lounge door, I saw independent me.

What freedom to be an entertainer, I wouldn't have to work at my father's fish market on the Wharf and endure that fishiness all day, but more than that—living and working close to my family meant a host of familial obligations that included the dreaded tribal ritual of Sunday dinners.

When my cousins, aunts, uncles and grandparents arrived

at our front door on Sunday afternoons, I wanted to rush up and bolt the overbearing tribe out. Everyone talked so emphatically, and no one listened—they were always trying to out-do each other. Why did they all have to be so loud and go on and on? I was told that in a big family, the code was 'he who speaks quietly is forgotten'. I put cotton in my ears to block out all that sibling rivalry.

When the family tribe took over our house in the Marina District on Sundays, they must have already prepared for the evening's battle plan and barely got their coats off before a skirmish broke out over the best time to plant tomatoes or whose turn it was to host Easter Sunday brunch. They never talked about anything I was interested in—they assumed that because they were having a good time, I should be too. The men eventually deferred any unresolved issues until the next Sunday dinner and retreated to the living room for whatever game was on television.

From that fateful New Year's on, when I thought of marriage, I envisioned endless Sundays in a continual losing battle with my big-bully cousin, vying for my favorite overstuffed chair in the privacy of a corner. If my parents had only foreseen that image of grown-up Tony singing and telling jokes in a casino lounge that flashed before my eyes, they would have taken the long way around to avoid that lounge door.

All Joe and Isabelle wanted to do was take me out for my birthday and catch a dinner show while they were at it, never imagining their son would formulate a subversive plan to escape the tyranny of family life every Sunday. They had no clue their boy woke up every Sunday morning plotting to avoid aunts who pestered him on details of his life or fight for repossession of the coveted overstuffed chair.

I discovered that if I looked miserable enough, which wasn't hard to do while sitting in a hardback chair stuck right in the middle of things, my aunts would flock about to feel my forehead, argue about what kind of medicine to give me and send me upstairs if, after a protracted discussion, they agreed I was unwell. Happy days.

Eventually, though, it dawned on me that if I was going to be an entertainer, I should stick around after dinner to listen to the stories and jokes about things that went on at the Wharf that week. Once I took the cotton out of my ears, I heard how funny a few of my relatives could be.

I memorized their delivery of jokes and practiced them in my room upstairs like they were gold to use as banter between songs in my future lounge routine. One night, just before the women were about to clear the table and disappear into the kitchen for more debates and dishwashing, I surprised everyone by popping out of my chair and asking if I could sing a few songs for them.

In response to the astonished look on everyone's face that this silent boy would want to entertain them, my father tried to explain, "Ever since Tony caught a few minutes of an act in the side lounge last year in Reno, he's wanted to sing and tell jokes."

"Ah, Tone" said Uncle Dom in his thick old-world accent, "you want to be a Lounge Lizard…you want the nightlife."

Everyone laughed as though Uncle Dom had said Tony wanted to live on the moon. However, I didn't laugh, I was electrified by the name Lounge Lizard, it sounded decadent, offbeat, and no one would invite a lizard of any kind to Sunday dinner.

The relatives exclaimed what a lovely voice I had, "so much

like Grandpa Gianni in his voice and the personality in the performance". My father smiled approvingly, "it's like you are a different person when you are singing, my boy, not at all that grumpy kid hiding out in that oversized chair." I wondered if my Great-Grandpa Gianni had ever wanted to be a lounge lizard and planned his getaway from Sunday dinners to be part of the bigger, broader, modern world.

I learned that daydreaming allowed me to turn down the volume on the mothers, sisters, and cousins all trying to be heard above the fray of dinner preparations. With their voices in the background, I wouldn't have to listen to Mom and Aunt Florinda argue about who got the better grades in school and never coming to an agreement—instead I was able to muse on what life would be like when I could stay out as late as he wanted.

In my daydreams, I could drink Ramos Fizzes for breakfast. The girls would say they liked my pencil-thin mustache and bright gold, monogrammed cufflinks. Best of all, in my dreams, people stopped talking and listened when I had something to say. I always had plenty of jokes written down in my back pocket to keep them entertained at the Palomino Club, and I would catch a glimpse of my debonair self in the mirror behind the bar as I proclaimed in a loud, magnanimous voice *'drinks on me for everyone'*.

Eventually, I got a job at one of the lesser-known Reno casinos as a lounge entertainer. The tips were generous, and women left their phone numbers for me—I was living the good life. Now that my escape was complete, I surprised myself by driving five hours to Sunday dinner once a month. What compelled me to revisit the scene of my miserable Sundays? In reflective moments behind the wheel, I began to see Joe and Isabelle in a more tolerant light, descendants of immigrants whose family ties kept them safe in the new world. I thought about how they had grown shorter while I had grown to over 6 feet, and I didn't have the heart to give them a bad time when I was looking down at the top of their balding heads.

I could now shake off my parents' old-fashioned advice with a tolerant smile. I even rather liked them when they weren't talking. How would they cope with the Sunday dinners getting smaller? I worried that my cousins weren't getting married and having babies like their parents did and already there were 3rd and 4th cousins at the table to fill in for closer family ties. The law of attrition was leaving extra tables and chairs stacked in the garage.

I still counted my lucky stars that I could stay out as late as I wanted, but that was mitigated by the hangovers I'd nurse at the Palomino with Fred's extra creamy Ramos Fizzes. The sound of dice cups hitting the bar on those hungover mornings hurt my head and with each pound reverberating between my temples I reminded myself I was living the dream.

Good life or not, once a month the thought of homemade ravioli and chicken called me back home. Sundays hadn't changed much, except I was not so easily annoyed. The women were older and a little slower now, but they still squabbled in the kitchen, and the men still rooted endlessly for their teams in the living room. Although I hadn't paid attention to sports before, I was now caught up in the energy and randomly picked a team to enjoy the comradery of cheering with my father, uncles and even older 2nd cousin.

One Friday morning I lit my girlfriend's first cigarette of the day, and as I blew out the match, heard myself asking if she'd like to drive to the San Francisco and have dinner at my parents' house on Sunday. I got a little dizzy at this suggestion and tried to recover by making it sound like a fun weekend on the town.

I told her that on Saturday we could go to Luigi's for dinner, they made terrific linguine and clams, and then go to a great neighborhood movie theater. In an attempt to make the weekend sound more familiar and enticing, I said that on Sunday morning we could visit Sal, a bartender we both knew, for a 'hair of the dog that bit us'. We could drive back Monday morning in time for work that evening. That was a much longer speech than I had anticipated.

She said, "Sure". Lenore was the only person he knew who could speak, chew gum, check her nails and smoke at the same time.

Lenore could not hold her liquor. When we went to Sal's for a 'hair of the dog', we stayed a little too long and she was tipsy—my uncles might call it 'blotto'. We were late and the homemade raviolis were gone by the time we arrived. Lenore's makeup was smudged, she was chain smoking, her bleached hair was extra ratted and piled high.

My mother trapped me in a back room. "Is this what you think of your father and me, bringing that floozie here?"

"Honestly Mom, she's alright, she doesn't usually have Mimosas for breakfast."

After much lecturing and finger-wagging, we returned to the living room and my mother let out a strangled cry of shock. Lenore had settled in on the couch with the men watching the game instead of being in the kitchen helping with the dishes and she seemed to be getting along famously with Grandpa.

I tried to stop laughing and my mother looked confused. "Mom, you really need to get out more."

Lenore looked up innocently and said, "What"? She had washed off her makeup and flattened her hair into tolerable proportions.

I became serious. "You just did the most wonderful thing, marry me."

Silence enveloped the room. Lenore stopped cheering for the 49ers, checked her nails, turned to me with her big smile and said, "Sure." There were polite murmurs all around, but when my mother retreated into the kitchen, I thought I heard "floozie" as the door swung closed.

The Road to Acrophobia

Acrophobia is the fear of heights, not a town on the road to Athens. I imagine my journey to this problem as heading up an ever-narrowing road to a mountain top where I could no longer deny that my well-intended aunts' predictions so many years ago came true.

The trip started at sea level where I spent part of my summers at the beach with my three fuss-budget aunts. 'Don't get too close, don't go too far. Stick to your side of the road. There's danger if you go off the path'. At the beach, this translated to'don't got too far out'.

They'd say things like, "you'll find out for yourself—the ribbon of highway that looks so inviting now and beckons you into to an endless horizon—that's an illusion. One day, they warned, my life would be as predictable as theirs.

Of course, I didn't believe them, they were sweet but silly old aunts who never went anywhere. Good thing they lived by the ocean, they didn't have to go far to be in a wonderful place. I didn't understand the grownups who lounged on the beach—I would charge joyously past them into the breakers and bob endlessly in the swells. I'd dive into a developing wave just before it broke; nothing compared to that buoyant feeling of timing it right and being swept up in the powerful flow.

Sometimes I'd miscalculate and a wave would crash hard on top of me and send me spinning into the sand, but apprehension of this was also thrilling. I'd emerge dripping wet and look at all the boring adults propped up like dolls on their beach chairs and colorful towels. I didn't get it. They might as well be in their living rooms. Who wouldn't want to bob in endless undulations and then get knocked about once in a while. They could chat and read anytime, and I swore that would never happen to me.

One strange day I did feel my life begin to narrow a bit. I loved my little red, inflatable raft, and I broke my aunts' inviolate rule to never go beyond the breakers. They had added, for extra effect to impress upon me to take heed, 'there are monsters out there'. I hadn't been tempted to go out there, it seemed too quiet and mysterious beyond the busy fun of the surf and swells.

On that day, however, I accidentally rode over the furthest swell and it nearly landed me on top of the strangest, giant, pink jellyfish that looked poised to sting me. I suddenly pictured more creatures that lived past the breakers— eels, squid, weird looking things, and others bigger than a car, and I didn't venture out into their world again. Looking back on it, that was when my aunts' prophecy began to take hold—I was now starting on the road to that place where an adult would rather sit safely in one spot and warn everyone else to take care.

Every summer I heard more admonitions about doing dangerous things. I only listened with one ear, but I did listen, and every year a few possibilities disappeared from that endless horizon I had seen before. Horses had been my friend, and they let you ride them too, but the aunts would say, 'it's too far to fall or, you might get kicked in the head'. Convertibles were the next best thing to horses, it felt so free with the wind in your hair, but 'what good's a roll bar, really.' Then there was swimming at the beach, my last refuge of freedom, but no, if there was any chance of lightning, even if the lifeguards said it was okay because there was none in the forecast; 'you never know'.

All it took to finish off my view of the endless road to a bright horizon were a few wrong turns and misadventures. I had already cut out singing, dancing and being a mathematician from life's possibilities. Then I was invited to Hawaii but thought of the mysterious silence beyond the breakers with giant pink jellyfish and car-sized monsters; I didn't want to fly two thousand miles over their territory. Actually, flying had already been crossed off my list of life's possibilities.

Instead of Hawaii, I decided to visit a friend in Colorado, so I hopped in my car and drove to the Rockies. Before I got to Glenwood Hot Springs, I wanted to see the view and pulled to the side of the road. The side of the mountain would be more accurate. There was gravel covering the shoulder, my tires lost traction, and the sliding didn't stop until the car was inches from the abyss.

Driving to Arrowhead Lake I didn't expect the drama of a cantilevered road extending out into the California sky from the rock-faced mountainside like a skinny little bridge thousands of feet over a canyon.

I also didn't expect the wind to buffet my car while on a crumbly, narrow two-lane road with no shoulder driving around blind turns on the way to the Ranger's Station at the summit of Mt Diablo. My skimpy sandals kept sliding off the clutch and I came close to passing out from holding my breath.

Equally disturbing was a trip to Mt Hamilton Observatory; it was okay unless you missed an unmarked turn into the parking lot and were greeted with a long, steep descent into the Sacramento Valley and a sign warning *Patterson, 50 miles.*

Apparently, I was alone in making that wrong turn and the asphalt looked dusty and forgotten. It wasn't wide enough to turn around and no one would think of looking for a car deep in that wild and isolated brushy canyon that bordered the road all the way to civilization.

Now, like my aunts before me, I enjoy my life within self-imposed confines. I am no longer a free spirit, frolicking on the beach, and I no longer travel on the ribbon of highway I envisioned years ago that led to an endless, golden horizon. I left that luminous path and found a predictable, rarified existence where dangers are filtered to a level tolerable for me.

I hope you understand when I say that although acrophobia isn't a town in Greece, it is a place that one inhabits. It keeps you within its perimeter and only lets you out on special occasions, and even then, when I scale its walls, I can hear my three aunt's admonitions 'don't go too far; don't go too high'.

Tokyo Time

In the mid-twentieth century, most Californians measured the age of a building or culture in years, not centuries. Unless you visited museums or historical sites to investigate the history of the Native Californians, Spanish missions or the gold rush, everything that you came across in daily life was relatively new.

By chance, I had the opportunity to spend a week in Japan, a different kind of world where juxtapositions of old and new put time out of joint—but in a good way. I was an art student and looked especially forward to seeing timeless Mt Fujii, the iconic centerpiece of so many Japanese prints.

After a 14-hour flight, I arrived with very clean hands thanks to the warm steamed towels presented at every meal. What a comforting tradition to hold those mini saunas in your hands. There we were on a jet plane flying 500 miles per hour halfway around the world and this little tradition was a welcome anachronism—a preview of things to come.

When the plane landed in Tokyo, I looked out the window and saw twenty men on bicycles coming out to meet the plane to unload the luggage. My memory is a little fuzzy about what else they did, but I thought it was charming and quaint.

Juxtapose that with the taxi driver in front of the airport who, without getting out of the cab, pushed a button on his dashboard and popped the back door open. He apologized for almost knocking me over. "Everyone in Tokyo knows to stand clear of the door". There was a bit of a language barrier and I'm not sure I understood him exactly, the point is, back then it was astonishing to make the back door open from the dash. Of course, a few years later that wouldn't be such a surprise and now cabs even drive themselves, but I still approach taxi doors with caution.

The driver took me to my hotel in the suburbs at the end of a subway line. Commuters with briefcases were emerging to ground level as we passed the station, and he said I could get downtown from that station. This was much like any other big city until we arrived at my hotel a few seconds later. There stood an awesome, moody dark-stone castle with a tiled and beamed roof that turned up at the corners. It was surrounded by a spacious, minimalist garden where a red, black and gold rooster proudly strutted on guard. I looked back down the street and less than a block from this timeless scene were businessmen still emerging from the subway entrance.

When the sun rose the next morning, the self-important rooster crowed louder than one would think possible—he managed this with considerable effort by becoming formidable, his chest puffed up, with his back and neck outstretched so all could hear him. He didn't know he was obsolete and that the businesspeople inside, making deals over their power breakfasts, had watches with fancy dials that showed the time all over the world—they didn't need to be told the sun was up.

I walked to the subway, then caught the new Bullet train that sped along frictionless tracks at a comfortable 200 miles an hour to the Shogun's Palace in Kyoto. I was speaking with a few of my fellow passengers who knew English when Mt Fuji loomed into sight in all its immutable glory.

I had seen many representations of that symbol of Japan and must have let my excitement show. The Japanese businessmen around me on their way to Kyoto smiled indulgently and said they forget to look. Even at 200 miles per hour, it took a long time to pass that big volcano, and I thought about the people who spent their entire lives in its shadow.

The Bullet train was a futuristic marvel that sped along on a pillow of air above the tracks, and it was disorienting to soon be walking the halls of the Shogun's Kyoto palace. One minute to be traveling in comfort at breakneck speed and the next to enter a silent, timeless world. It wasn't hard to imagine the Shogun's guards listening in the quiet night for an intruder's footsteps to make the nightingale floorboards sing. Outside the palace, the scenes were almost indistinguishable from old woodblock prints I'd seen with cormorants standing on a stone bridge looking for fish.

Then it was back on the Bullet train to speed past the immutable Mt Fuji from the opposite direction and I thought I saw a man in a field painting yet another interpretation of the mountain cast in the light of yet another setting sun.

Later in the week I took an air-conditioned tour bus, the coolness a welcome treat in the humid rainy season, to a few ancient villages, each one specializing in a single craft. The economy of one village was largely based on the dying of textiles, where workers bent over ancient stone dye vats dug into the ground. A second village relied on a factory that manufactured popular red, black and white 'good luck' dolls. I watched a woman paint an eye on doll after doll, leaving one eye blank for the purchaser to fill in when a wish was made.

The next day was a trip to ultramodern Dreamland, a

smaller version of Disneyland, but with a Japanese take on the characters, followed by a personally guided tour of downtown Tokyo's Ginza district at night—the Ginza was like a theme park for adults with activities for every appetite and lit as brightly as Times Square.

The week was a blur. Japan has been called the 'Floating World' for its dream-like qualities and floating in my mind was a phantasmagorical wheel of images. Cormorants on a stone bridge looking for fish, followed by the neon Ginza at night, a silent Buddhist temple in the middle of a noisy city, and the rooster guarding my castle, bravely willing to challenge any intruders from the subway next door. Many centuries circled in my mind's eye, with the timeless Mt Fuji at the center presiding overall.

I didn't want to leave, but modern life was calling from across the ancient Pacific, so I said goodbye to Tokyo and rewound my journey by leaving the broodingly dark stone castle, watching the bicycles head back to the airport from the plane, enjoying my warm towel hand sauna, arriving at the San Francisco airport with their big, unsurprising taxis and home to my waterbed. I looked at the beside clock and could almost hear the rooster crowing in Tokyo time; I hoped the businesspeople at the hotel appreciated his efforts, distracted as they were with big deals and world watches.

Twins

I didn't want anything to go wrong, not on our last day as business partners—I was already planning what retirement would look like, and it didn't include my twin brother, Ethan. He was the captain, and I was the tour guide for the June Emberly, our whale watching boat named after our mother. Our uncle gave us the boat, but our mother said there was one stipulation, that my twin brother Ethan and I would have to get along. I'm a people person, and my brother is not, and that's why my job was to keep passengers on an even keel, while his job was to do the same with the boat. We argued a lot, but the one thing we agreed on was to honor our mother's wish that we work well together, and we managed to run the most popular excursion boat at the marina.

People always said, 'you two are nothing alike'. But they hadn't seen how time had warped us. Seventy years of living carved Ethan's face into a tragedian mask, a man obliged to go down with his excursion boat. He had spartan habits and looked dehydrated because he lived on a little ale, boiled meat, potatoes and gruel.

He wore a still-dark, straight, full beard that fanned from ear to ear, and a turned-down mouth that coordinated with his perpetual frown. His face was tanned and creased from spending his days on the bow—searching, always searching. He said he was looking for whales, but to me it seemed more a habit that kept him from looking inward or to avoid people.

Ethan developed cataracts from all those years of staring into the glare of sun and sea and this gave his eyes a mysterious opaqueness that added to his already enigmatic persona. The older he got, the longer and more outrageous his fanned-out beard became, the more mysterious his cataracts made him look, and his imperious attitude grew more imposing. Customers began commenting that he was more like a fictional, larger than life sea captain like Moby Dick's Captain Ahab than one would expect to find on an excursion boat.

My face—I'm not proud of it—has barely more gravitas than Santa Claus. If I had a theatrical mask, it would be that of the smiling comedian. All my life I've been sociable and indulged in good food and wine. I've always used sunblock, protected my eyes with sunglasses—no cataracts for me—and I'm clean-shaven with rosy cheeks. People call me Santa because I look like him if the big elf wore a fisherman's hat and cable knit sweater and because they say I'm always jolly.

Lately, Ethan's been even more cantankerous and spending more time looking out to sea. A therapist friend once said, "Ethan is looking for his long-lost mother—the whale is an obvious mother figure." That was the one time I can remember Ethan and I both laughing out loud together. We said, in unison, "You Freudians are always talking about mothers!" But did we protest too much? It was a strange coincidence that our mother, who swam regularly in the ocean with an aquatic club, disappeared one day in a rip tide.

How could they see the similarities between Captain Ahab and Santa. There are, however, things we secretly admired about each other. I give much of the credit for our success to my brother and his mystifying affinity with the whales and his reputation for having this whale-sense usually filled our boat to capacity.

I knew my brother wished he could be more sociable like me. Unfortunately, he could never wipe that frown off his face to make pleasant conversation—that was one of my abilities, to be friendly and make it a fun trip whether we found a whale or not. I knew how to entertain the passengers and gave them a running commentary on what we were doing as well as a fair share of puns and seafaring jokes.

Our mother said we were only identical less than a month before the differences appeared. "People couldn't tell you apart until your personalities made you look different. Bobby had a sunny disposition and smiled every time you looked at him. I'm sorry Ethan, but a cross, frowning baby is not cute and cuddly. What we thought was a morose expression I found was just your thinking face that you have to this day. You acted like a grumpy, genius adult and that made people nervous, so you were left in the shadows and watched as Bobby was picked up, cooed at, and bounced on visitor's knees.

One day, when you both were in the crib I saw you, Ethan, staring at your brother like you were trying to figure out what there was about him that got all the attention. There were tears in your eyes, but you didn't cry out loud, you just frowned, so I picked you up, held you close, and you melted in my arms."

When we turned 18, our mother said, "Boys, your uncle is retiring and wants to give you his excursion boat, and I want you to learn how to work out your differences and make a success out of the business. To do that you must respect each other."

We said in unison, "I don't know, being stuck on a boat with him every day wouldn't work."

Ethan said, "what if I want to go to Harvard?"

I said, "I was thinking of trying to make it on Broadway."

"Please try it for a year, I think you would be good for each other."

If our mother only knew that in some ways her plan would work out for the business side of things, but personally, we had become more different and annoyed with each other than ever. I was glad this was our last trip out together—I was getting older, and Ethan's pigheadedness was becoming intolerable— he seemed more willing to take chances just as I was becoming more fearful of the sea. I thought he was either showing off for attention in the final days of our seafaring venture, or perhaps he was indeed transforming into a version of Captain Ahab and taking the whale quest too seriously.

On the days when the whales were elusive and he was on a mission to go further out to find one, it was my job to keep Ethan in check and ensure he returned us back to the marina safely. I thought of myself as the buffer between Ethan and the passengers and I was also the glue that kept each day's band of disparate strangers from becoming a ship of fools—outsized personalities can be magnified in a confined vessel bouncing around on the ocean.

My brother's job was to use his finely tuned whale-sense to intuit where they would be and to time it for them to breach and slap the water with their tail. That's what the people came for, but lately I had lost confidence in his judgement, instead of thinking about the good of everyone on board, he was more determined to impress them with.

One day he absolutely promised to find them a whale and he should never have done that. Deaf to the passengers' complaints that they wanted to get back to shore before dark, he kept the boat out past sunset. He excused this by saying that he 'wanted them to see the mighty beast' he had promised them. He never used to talk like he is in a Victorian novel and that's when I was convinced more than ever it was time to retire.

He was also becoming less patient and more cantankerous. One day, two kids were running on the deck and before I could corral them, he stepped out of the wheelhouse and literally growled at them and at the mother. The mother became slightly hysterical at Ethan's tone and threatened to complain to the marina that the captain was unfit to command the excursion boat. It was my job to keep the peace, mollify her, to explain that he was the best whale watching captain on the west coast and just having a bad day. We were lucky that she calmed down, huffily accepted her refunded money and still got to see the whales.

There I was again, first mate, tour guide and peacekeeper for my difficult, genius brother who got away with behaving badly. At times like this I admit, I was jealous of my brother. I had to work so hard to make everyone happy, it was my job to always think of the other person, while he could bluster through life and step on people's feelings without suffering for it. I honored our mother's wishes that fateful night our uncle gave us the boat and she made us swear to be civil and make things work between us while he took it for granted. What would happen to us now that we wouldn't have the boat as a common focus.

All was right with the world this morning though—except there were more than the usual number of chattering seagulls lined up on the marina and more were coming in from the ocean. This could be taken for a sailor's warning that there was a storm brewing out there, but I didn't know if I had the heart to call off this last trip, especially since looking out to sea there was nothing to indicate the weather was about to turn from such a fine day. A week before, a fishing boat was almost caught in a squall that had come up from the tropics, but I shrugged it off, it was a rare occurrence here and this was our last day.

Despite more seagulls lining up on the dock railing, everything was calm in the marina. Little whisps of fog had lifted and the sun created colorful reflections of boats on the water, the glassy surface only disturbed by the complicated ripples that only a paddling duck could make.

Passengers started arriving and I tried to ignore a few more seagulls coming in from the ocean. A troop of 2nd graders got on board. There were more of them than I expected, but I could tell the chaperones had them well in hand. Everybody got a life jacket, including the frail-looking older couple that came aboard holding hands.

I hoped the kids and the couple could tolerate the motion of the sea. I figured we'd shove off after a young lady slowly made it up the ramp—she was having a heated discussion with someone on her cell phone and stopped every time it was her turn to talk. I told her to refrain from using her phone onboard and she nodded but kept her phone to her ear— I wouldn't miss people like that.

We had been waiting for two more people, but it was already a few minutes past scheduled departure. It was time to start the engines and leave when I saw a man and a woman stumbling across the parking lot. His hair was flamboyantly long, salt and pepper, while hers cropped spiky short and bleached. As they negotiated the ramp, I thought they looked like wild cards, not a good thing on a boat, especially on the last day—I didn't want anything to go wrong.

When I recognized him, it was even worse, this was Ricky Gamberini, a rock star who, 20 years earlier, had been notorious for tearing up hotel rooms and once threw hotel furniture out a window. I knew he lived in town, and he appeared to be reliving past glory days. I checked to see if his friend was carrying a flask in her purse—his skinny jeans were so tight he couldn't hide a Kleenex, much less a bottle. I sternly informed them there was no alcohol on board and they took that well, although they seemed a little too animated to be running on just their own biochemistry. She stumbled and he laughed too loudly, and I wondered what they had fortified themselves with before getting on board. I thought of the vulnerable 2nd graders and reminded myself that even a Santa Claus-like first mate had a legal right to physically subdue a passenger. I was 70, but I was still big, strong and not impaired with whatever they had in their system.

I had given Ethan the high sign to take off and was curious what the delay was. He was acting stranger than usual, and I figured he was emotional about this being the last trip. I had already told people the rules and regulations and made sure everyone had their life jackets on correctly when my brother surprised me by stepping out of the wheelhouse, introducing himself and repeating a few of the rules that I had just said. Then he made that dreaded promise, that we would find a whale come hell or high water. Oh Ethan, I thought, I told you not to make grandiose promises like that. Thank goodness this was the last day.

After this display of hubris, Ethan was about to withdraw back into his wheelhouse sanctuary where no one could bother him, when Ricky Gamberini started up the ladder to the upper deck. My brother immediately saw Ricky's careless demeaner as a possible threat to safety on the boat; his wild appearance alone was a red flag. He had an expensive German camera dangling insecurely off his belt and it came loose when he was near the top of the ladder. It crashed into expensive pieces on the deck below—I wasn't surprised by Ricky's nonchalant reaction to the broken camera—I could almost read his mind, 'what's a few hundred bucks, I'm rich and I can always get a new one' but my brother was in disbelief.

I could read Ethan's mind too, 'Is that man in charge of his faculties? Someone like that should not be on a small boat'.

My brother growled a warning to me and then to Ricky, but I had more confidence in Ricky, I felt I knew him after following his escapades over the years. I had read he wasn't performing anymore and had started a music school. There was no furniture to trash on the boat; these days he looked like he couldn't pick up any furniture, much less throw it.

Ricky came over to me and said, "Hey man, that captain's a real jerk."

I smiled and agreed with him. He said, "Hey man, mind if I go down below and catch a quick nap?

"Of course not, go ahead," I said, relieved that he was voluntarily removing himself from the scene. He went over and told his girlfriend where he'd be and joked with the kids for a few minutes. The girlfriend had made friends with one of the chaperones and was helping with the kids.

We headed out to sea about 15 miles. I figured I'd been worried about nothing, but then another seagull came streaking past us for shore. I looked up and there was a freak squall that appeared out of nowhere; it hadn't been on the radio or on my cell phone.

If that wasn't bad enough, I could hear the engine had stopped running.

There's nothing worse than being struck sideways by high winds, especially a squall. I should have heeded the wisdom of the gulls, but I wanted this last day to be perfect, so I had turned a blind eye. I should have had the engine checked, but since this was our last trip out, it didn't seem necessary. Bad decision.

The marina hadn't radioed us about the squall. I ran to the wheelhouse where my brother was frantically trying to throttle the engine back into life.

"Get everyone down below," he screamed.

I was already on my way, herding little kids and the surprised looking older couple into the cabin below. I had to grab the cell phone away from the young lady to get her downstairs, and she gave me a 'how dare you' look until I pointed to the black cloud on the horizon that was heading our way and moving fast. She grabbed her phone back and ran into the cabin.

I could hear Ethan's attempts to revive the engine so we could either turn and face the wave and wind at a better angle, or if he got it started soon, maybe we could get out of its path entirely. It didn't look very wide, but it was very dark and there was big a flash of lightning inside it. What's a first mate to do at this point, it was all up to Evan, the brother who had always been the genius.

There was a gut-wrenching silence as Evan stopped throttling to avoid flooding the engine with gas; I knew he was waiting until the last minute for the engine to recover and I was glad the others were down below so they couldn't see the squall bearing down on the June Emberly. The advance wind and rain were coming directly at our side, an angle that could mean disaster once the main part of the squall hit. Just when I grabbed the railing and braced for impact the engine chugged to life, the boat jerked forward a foot, then started with a roar that could barely be heard above the oncoming wind.

If the engine didn't give out, I knew Ethan would get us through this like a real heroic sea captain, not just a fictional one. He headed at a 30-degree angle into the wave that would have hit us broadside in a minute if the engine hadn't started. He motored slowly against the strong wind and over the top of a big wave, then pulled the throttle back hard so we wouldn't plunge down the other side. We continued like this for another few minutes until we came out on the other side of the squall.

In relief, Ethan and I looked at each other with mutual regard. We were both red in the face, drenched and windblown, but we made it without capsizing the boat. I didn't want to think about the enormity of what could have happened. I ran to the cabin below and the children were excited and a little scared, but the adults, including Ricky Gamborini, ex-furniture throwing rock star, and his girlfriend were helping keep everything in hand.

That extraordinary event did something to Ethan, it released him from that mask of tragedy he always wore; I had forgotten what he looked like until the corners of his mouth turned up instead of down and the furrows in his forehead relaxed. He smiled shyly as everyone congratulated him on his expert skills and I barely recognized him. Had he been in self-imposed isolation in the wheelhouse all these years because he didn't want to show that he was just an ordinary person, not a larger-than-life Captain Ahab or not even lovable like his brother.

The passengers were all over him with pats on the back and one of the older chaperones handed him a slip of paper with her phone number on it. Ricky got a kick out seeing the old captain get a lady's phone number.

On the other hand, I was wearing a frown as I thought about the drama, the danger I had put us in; I saw it was all my fault—I hadn't the good sense to heed the seagulls warning and to get the engine serviced. I'd put my wishes that our last day working together be perfect and to save for retirement instead of getting the engine serviced. When I saw my reflection in the cabin mirror, the concern showed on my face—my eyebrows were furrowed, and I was not smiling.

Ricky's punk girlfriend was a better host than I was on that trip—she found cups, coffee and cocoa and we all stood sipping our hot drinks. One of the kids had been staring at us as he peered over his cup of cocoa and asked, "Hey, are you two twins?"

The Arizona Room

It was the end of May and wind howled down the loop off Lake Michigan so hard it undid the chin ties of my hat and blew it onto the icy street. Cars careened left and right and spun around on the slippery street, and in peril of his life, George valiantly retrieved it. When he hopped back onto the pavement and caught his breath, he asked if we should give moving to Phoenix, Arizona a second thought—where the winters were ice-free and the grandchildren close by.

"Can we leave tomorrow?"

'Get in touch with nature', that was a mantra during the 60's. It wasn't the 60s anymore, but the mentality was still appealing. Proponents of this said that we are all children of nature, animals at heart, and we need to spend time outdoors and experience the wild, explore the woods, sail down the coast with only our wits and the stars to guide us. We never had that luxury, for us it was babies and work, work, work, and to our surprise we had gotten old to the point where a simple walk in May down Michigan Avenue became treacherous to our now fragile bones.

We chose a place on the outskirts of Phoenix at the interface of the desert and a housing development that had been built just a few years before. Apparently, the wildlife didn't get the message that the senior community wasn't theirs to roam freely anymore, there was a new species in town. A wide greenway ran behind the houses on our street and there was another row of houses on the other side of the greenway. Beyond that, there was a lettuce field and then the desert stretched to the mountains. It was lovely and we were very pleased with ourselves that first night as we sipped our G&T, watching the red and gold sun set behind purple mountains. The future was ours to command.

It was then that our legs began to feel like they were on fire, there was something invisible and biting that lived in that grass and they had discovered we were there. There was nothing to swat away, but we had been told about 'No See Ums', little natty things that were small enough to get through normal window screens by landing on the opening of a mesh and stepping through.

We would figure it out later and retreated in a hurry to the Arizona room. In the old days, everyone in Arizona had a room like this, the first line of defense against the outdoors. It's a walled-in room attached to the back of the house with big windows so that you felt like you were outside, but without the No See Ums setting your legs on fire. It wasn't quite like being in nature, but for us Chicagoans, it was close enough.

The next day, in-between applying liberal doses of anti-itch cream to my legs, I was pushing furniture back and forth in the living room when I heard my husband call from the den.

"Hey, look here. What do you think they needed this for?" He opened a built-in cabinet for me to see an empty rifle rack. I suggested that maybe the previous owners liked to go hunting somewhere far away, but it did seem odd, why was it in the living room—in Chicago that would be more a set up for someone prepared for a shootout.

That night we managed to get some sleep after my husband finally won the battle with a giant mosquito that sounded like a little motorcycle trying to drive into our ears.

"It's a tie, Arizona bugs score one, we score one".

I said, "we'll see what happens tomorrow." I turned off the light.

I lay awake listening for the ominous whine of a second-string mosquito.

"Guess we better keep the windows and doors closed if we want to get any sleep," said my husband"

"Right," I said, "and stay in the Arizona room for our cocktails if we don't want a repeat of yesterday's 'No See Um' attack."

Breakfast was everything we had envisioned our retirement home to be. The farmhouse style kitchen had a cheerful, bright window with the sun at an oblique angle so we wouldn't get sunburned while eating. Outside, we had a view of a colorful plant that was in full bloom and its orange flowers contrasted beautifully with the bluest sky that looked straight out of a watercolor box.

"Ah, that was nice," we both agreed, "it's much more relaxing when you are safe behind a window looking at the beauty."

I said, "I'm going to get a few linens out of the duffel bag in the closet."

"What? Oh, right, the light is out in the closet, I'll fix it in a minute."

I went into the bedroom closet humming a little tune. I had visions of playing golf and all the things I didn't have time to do all those years of work-work-work. There was barely any light in the closet, but I knew what I wanted and reached into the open duffle and took out a couple of sheets for the spare room, then I reached in again—just as my hand was about to grab for another sheet I saw a large, shadowy prehistoric outline that looked like the pictures of geckos I had seen—at least a foot long. This was much bigger than what I had imagined, and I let out a little scream. I was shaking as I zipped up the duffel, ran past my husband who was still engrossed in the newspaper and out the door to the front yard, unzipped the bag and turned the creature loose. I watched as the it ran as fast as it could under the house— no, I thought, not under the house, go far away please! There was a utility worker high up on a pole across the street and he had witnessed the scenario—an old lady freaked out by gecko—and he was laughing so hard I had to laugh too.

My husband arrived on the front porch and said, "What in the world is so hilarious?"

"Well, for one thing, I think there is a gecko, maybe a gecko family, that lives under our house."

"Well,", he said, "no one has lived in this house for a while, so things will get better once these critters know they don't have run of the place."

If only that were true. For the next few weeks, we were treated to doves copulating every day on our decorative garden bridge in the front yard. We referred to it as lover's lane; every time we looked out the window, there they were. It surely must have been many different doves, but they all looked alike. At first it was cute.

Our kids and grandkids came over not long after we had moved in. They lived in a development on the far side of town where wildlife had been evicted and I had told them to wear long sleeves and pants if they wanted to go on our patio.

We were having dinner when a grandson looked out the window and said, "Look, there's a herd of rabbits!"

My husband said with a wink, "Do you call a bunch of rabbits a herd? I don't know. We see 15-20 rabbits running across the street every day, don't you?"

After dinner we all sat around the kitchen table because the living room couches had been fumigated. Our daughter was cleaning up the kitchen and asked,

"Where's the garbage barrel?"

"Oh, do you see that round, metal cover in the side yard by the sidewalk? You lift the lid and drop the trash bag into it. On Mondays, before school, a garbage truck slowly drives down the street and teenage boys run alongside it."

"What?"

"The boys, one on each side of the truck, open the lids in the yards on both sides of the street, pull the metal barrels out of the ground and empty them into the back of the truck. They replace the barrels, then run to follow the truck down the street to the next houses. An above ground source of food in this neighborhood would not last an hour. I put things that won't go down these dried-out disposal pipes in the freezer until Monday."

"I've never heard of anything like that!" She said.

The sun was low in the sky after dinner when the kids went to the patio, but they were soon back.

"There's five coyotes coming down the greenway!"

My son-in-law and daughter didn't believe them, "They're probably big dogs," and they ran to look from the safety of the Arizona room window. My husband and I just sat at the table; nothing would surprise us. We had already seen coyotes lounging around on our community golf course while people played past them. One of the golfers said that it's like alligators in Florida where he had seen a groundskeeper put orange cones not too far away from a gator as a warning."

We finally got up to see, and there they were, five scraggly coyotes that looked like they could use a good meal trotting past our Arizona room window. My daughter, who has enough courage for the rest of us, went out to see where the coyotes were going, and she called us out to take a look. Down a few houses on the greenway, a tiny white-haired lady waved a big white sheet at the coyotes. The coyotes stopped in their tracks, edging a little forward, then a little back as if in retreat. It looked like a dance. Apparently confused about what to do next, they stood for a few minutes looking at each other as though conferring. They agreed not to challenge that strange flapping sheet and, looking hangdog and hungry, slowly retraced their steps past our Arizona room windows, out into the desert and the developing shadows of evening.

The beautiful quail were a treat. On cue, every morning with the rising of the sun, they would hop on the window boxes underneath the sun-reflective windows of the Arizona room and peck at their reflection. I set up an easel so I could stand on the other side of the window, paint their fine markings and watch their behavior. Not long after that, 12 fluffy baby quail chicks, hardly bigger than a half-dollar, came toddling out from an old, overgrown bush by the house that we had planned on discarding. They had trouble getting through the grass, but mom and dad were patient. One day, the quail family had left, or were taken, hard to tell.

We admitted defeat, real nature was too much for us city people. Our children and grandchildren spent every weekend outdoors and accepted nature for what it is, and I am proud of them. Now my husband and I live in a glass ivory tower high above Phoenix. We think of it as an elevated Arizona Room where we can use our imagination to curate our view of the desert that stretches to the mountains. We have quail figurines living on the window ledge. We have coffee table books and guidebooks about nature, we watch nature shows on television, contribute to water conservation groups and the Audubon Society in memory of those quail that woke us every morning. Every now and then, while on high alert for rattlers, we take short hikes with the family among mindboggling stone formations. We applaud the setting sun while we picnic in our penthouse Arizona Room.

It's perfect.

Tangerine

1943

The explosion had been so close to Eddy that it left him legally blind, and his friend had convinced him he needed to get out and attend a USO dance. This was his first foray into a social situation since his life had been upended and he was having trouble getting his bearings in the crowded room. Even though the room was well lighted, this adventure was perhaps ill-advised; people kept moving around and it took effort to make sense of what he was looking at. He relied on light and shadow to give form to things and when people didn't stand still, he didn't have time to decipher shapes.

His retinas preserved some of the warm colors around him so that things either appeared dark with reflected light or with shades of orange and yellow. He blinked hard, trying to engage his eyes to focus and get a good look at a lady who was standing very still and sharing a joke with his friend. Her calmness was a beacon and his connection to her centered him among the swirling people—was he staring at her too long?

He looked away and struggled again to organize light and shadow in the room into coherent shapes. He tried channeling the poised, calm lady and it helped—the more relaxed he felt, the more light he could see and the moving figures were easier to follow. Forms began coalescing into recognizable patterns, colors floated out of the dimness in random places, but he was thankful for the orange tones that remained in his vision, even if the sunny brightness they represented was not very accurate. It was like a late Monet painting he once saw in which old Monet's failing retinas played tricks on him and he painted his garden at Giverny in implausible yellow, purple and brown tones when his earlier paintings of the garden were greens, reds and blues.

The lights in the USO Hall had an ochre, yellow glow and the calm lady's lipstick shined a bright tangerine color floating in the charcoal dark and light tones of the room. Like old Monet's retinas, his own were relaying unusual things to him, but it didn't matter, this sunrise color cheered him.

Even though Eddy had only been out of the hospital a few weeks and was testing his social skills prematurely, he responded to the visual drama of the real world—everything in the hospital was bathed in a uniform, flat, dull light that reduced contrasting reflections and shapes. It was uninspiring.

Eddy decided he had acted nonchalantly for an acceptable period of time and looked in the woman's direction again while she was distracted talking to his friend and her husband. Her composure appeared to have the same effect on others that she had on him; they were drawn to her calmness and circled around her, possibly hoping that some of it wear rub off on them.

He wanted to talk to her, but he didn't know how to behave anymore. Could he be charming like his old self while he was operating at such a disadvantage? Could he connect with people? Could he dance? When he lost his vision, he had trouble seeing inside himself too. Who was he? He still had ideas to share and things he wanted to do. He had always gravitated toward the company of people. Eddy was unaware that he was still staring her and she turned toward him, her petite outline shining reflected ambient light and her encouraging smile was bright tangerine.

Eddy navigated his way to her past a couple of dancers. "Would you like to dance?"

"Are you sure?" she asked with those neon lips.

She sounded hesitant, probably worried he would trip and fall. He had become a better dancer since he lost most of his sight, the physical therapists had him moving around in space and dancing every day.

"I was more likely to trip over my own feet before," he shouted over the music

"Uh-huh, well, let's give it a go," she shouted back.

The center of the floor suddenly parted as confused-looking dancers saw the young man with a white cane under his arm dancing the Fox Trot and then the cha-cha. They soon regained the floor, more confident they wouldn't be stepped on by the unusual twosome. The tempo of the music changed, and they slow-danced to *So Rare* and then of all things, the band played Jimmy Dorsey's *Tangerine*.

Eddy sensed the husband hovering nearby and he wanted to show he was in charge of himself, so he bid the lady goodnight, looking straight into her glimmering corneas that floated above bright, upturned lips and said, "you are my beacon". Before he could get tapped on the shoulder, with surprising agility and a little luck, he made it without incident back to the refreshment table where everything smelled like citrus.

Earthquake Weather

October is one of the best, if not the best month of the year in California. It arrives with cool nights that bring out the hidden colors in leaves, it sends the fog out to the sea and brings a short, mild second summer. It feels like a respite, a time to take stock and plan. It invites you to find an hour to relax, put your face in the lingering sun and gather strength for the winter ahead.

Oddly enough, this same gentle month is associated with a suppressed anxiety about the earth being violently knocked from under your feet and every fall someone can be counted on to say, 'it's so nice out…earthquake weather'! How this unfounded idea became so embedded in California psyche is a mystery, but still it persists. Maybe it's the knowledge that there is no such thing as perfection in nature, so if it's a perfectly fine autumn day, something might happen.

October can be nostalgic but bittersweet; if it had a voice it would whisper, 'it's beautiful today, but winter's coming, make your plans now'. Years of evolution has taught us to not trust winter—it tells us it's a season for survival, and relatively easy California living does not undo that intuition.

Each year around this time I nagged Ralph about moving back to the city from the suburbs and each year I'd try a new tack.

"Ralph, we've lived on this suburban street for 30 years, all our friends have left, and we are the only ones of our generation hanging on here."

"Eh, so? He grunted. Ralph did not like change.

I was expecting this monosyllabic answer and was not discouraged. I know change is unsettling, but I wanted to work, do city things, breathe city air and smell the ocean. I thought if I worked in the city, the commute would become so unbearable and I would complain so much about it, Ralph would want to move to keep me from going on about it. Convoluted, I know, but 30 years of marriage can teach you not to approach things head on—it's often better to sneak up on a subject.

Since Ralph was retired, I bolstered my argument for moving back to the city by pointing out the advantages of a second income. I told him that the best offer I had was a teaching position at San Francisco State. The school was only 35 miles aways but funneling rush hour traffic into the tunnel and over jammed bridges, the actual drive time was one and a half hours each way. Ralph said there must be something closer, and he was right, but I had San Francisco on my mind. I could get dinner in the city to avoid the traffic, especially on the evenings when there were exhibition openings, that kind of thing. I could fill up on wine and cheese and head home. It made me feel young again to think I might have to wear something besides sandals and jeans.

It was October 17th, 1989, and the day was perfect—warm, clear and exceedingly quiet, like the weather was holding its breath for something to happen. I kissed Ralph on the cheek and said, "I'm going to see the head of the math department "I'll be back by 6:30 at the latest, but I'm aiming for 6:00."

"Good," he replied, "because I just remembered the

grandkids are being dropped off here at 4:00 for a sleepover. They like my spaghetti."

The guilt started to rise in my chest, but I pushed it back down, "Ralph, this will be good for both of us."

Ralph grunted. "But I'll miss you."

"Nice try, you'll miss my cooking dinner three nights a week."

He grunted again.

So romantic, I thought. When did he start grunting all the time? If something doesn't change, I'll be grunting too.

I popped my favorite mixed tape into the tape deck and headed down winding, empty streets past houses that 30 years ago looked like identical ranch-style houses but over the years owners put their own personalities into it and now you wouldn't guess they all had nearly identical floorplans.

Finally, I was on 680, heading for the inevitable traffic jam at the entrance to the tunnel that separated the suburbs from the more developed East Bay. Often, thanks to the East Bay hills holding the marine influence back, a driver would enter the tunnel in glorious sunshine and come out the other end in thick, dripping fog. Not in October though—then it's beach weather on the San Francisco side of the hills.

Once that tunnel hurdle was passed, there was the Bay Bridge to negotiate, or if the traffic was backed up almost to the tunnel, there was the choice of heading west to the friendlier Richmond-San Rafael bridge. The commuter would likely pay the price for that break in traffic at the SFR Bridge when they hit the jam-ups again on Highway 1 that goes over the Golden Gate Bridge. Once across this next to last hurdle, there is only the clogged artery of 19th Avenue that moves people to and from the Avenues. Passing the exit to the Presidio, I made a mental note to go to a member's party I read about next week if I got the job. Just like the old days, I thought, so many things to do. My mixed tape had tangled into an impossible knot, but the commute was almost over—only a half hour to go and I'd be in the personnel office.

The Department Chair took me to the cafeteria for a late breakfast and I was able to convince him that I'd kept up my degree in math over the years by tutoring upper division students at the local high school. Things went so well that he offered me the opportunity to replace a teacher who didn't know a quadratic equation from a hole in the ground and could I start next week teaching algebra and geometry to freshmen. After filling out a dozen personnel forms in triplicate, I headed straight for the library to spend the day catching up on my math skills.

By noon I had a major headache—remembering this stuff was not the breeze I thought it would be. I did some grunting of my own each time I turned the page to a new chapter. It was almost 5:00 when I looked up at the clock, slapped my forehead in a 'where does the time go' gesture. I didn't want to be late for Ralph and the girls, and it wouldn't be a good sign that I could handle the commute and home life. I reached for the stack of books piled high on the table to check out downstairs, but there were so many I couldn't carry them all to the car. I left half the books, no problem, I'd be back in a day or two for the rest of them, I was pretty confident there wouldn't be a rush on trigonometric analysis.

There was no line at the checkout desk, and I was filling out a form for a library card when the building jolted so hard it knocked the pen out of my hand. The concrete walls made a terrible wrenching noise, shuddered, and then everything lifted up and down. Then it did it again. A giant crack streaked across the wall opposite me. I couldn't believe that this five story, cement library, a monument to permanence, was bouncing up and down and sideways. Plaster and asbestos dust filled the air.

The young lady behind the counter stood frozen like a statue with the date stamp poised in midair, ready to check out the next book. Judging by the Midwest accent she'd greeted me with, she probably never had the existential experience of the ground shaking beneath her feet. Californians had been through this before, but this time it was big. People were running past the checkout desk to the front doors for the relative safety of the Quad, but she stood there immobilized, her eyes wide. I pulled the date stamp out of her hand and clapped until she blinked. I shouted, "Earthquake... run!" She suddenly got the picture and beat me out the door because I was carrying all those books—I had a twinge of guilt because I hadn't checked them out, but I knew there'd be plenty of time before that building opened its doors again.

I was panicky entering the multitiered parking structure—I thought it might collapse at any moment and the term 'flattened' came to mind. I was hyperventilating by the time I made it out of the parking garage to 19th Avenue where automobiles were motionless in both directions for miles. No traffic lights were working on 19th Avenue and it was the main road to the Golden Gate Bridge from the Sunset District.

Okay, I thought, I'd get off 19th and head over to the Bay Bridge, but the radio said that bridge had collapsed. In reality, it was one section of the top tier that collapsed, killing an unfortunate woman who should have left work a few seconds earlier. I'm guessing she'd seen the gap opening before eyes. I don't know what I would have done in that split second, but instead of slamming on the breaks and hoping for the best, she gunned her car to sail over the gap like a stunt person. It didn't work. She was not the only person to lose their life that day.

The availability of personal cell phones was only a dream at the time and landline service in San Francisco was nonexistent that night. My family heard that the Bay Bridge had collapsed, instead of saying it was a section of it, and since I was due to be on the bridge around that time, they were convinced I was at the bottom of the bay under a pile of rubble.

I had mixed feelings when, in the early morning hours, it was my turn to drive onto the bridge. The Golden Gate Bridge was x-rayed for cracks and by midnight automobiles were allowed to start crossing, but I didn't want to think what an impossible challenge that would be to look for damage after dark on a windy bridge in a few hours. I held my breath; it was the same hair-raising sensation I had in the parking structure. It felt like when I was a kid at summer camp—when it was my turn to walk to the end of the high diving board. I couldn't make myself jump and crawled in chagrin back to the ladder and made all the grumbling kids in line behind me back down. That wouldn't work this night and I inched the car along onto the bridge.

I made it to Sausalito where the pay phones were working, and I called home. So much drama you'd think I was calling from the great beyond—the children were jumping up and down because they had heard about the bridge 'collapsing' and Ralph was so overcome he didn't grunt once.

By the following October we were settled in our old San Francisco neighborhood. My convoluted plan had worked! Ralph got tired of me complaining about the three hours on the freeway roundtrip. Then too, I was away so much, he looked around and finally noticed he was surrounded by bright-eyed young families at the starting gate.

Many places we had known in the city were gone, but there were enough to take their place, and we figured the earth wouldn't rumble like that again for a while. It's only in October, when the weather is perfect—warm and still, the Liquidambar trees a patchwork of yellow-magenta, and the fog is far out in the ocean that I think about earthquake weather and am wary of making big plans for the day.

DESSERT AND BRANDY

Isha Says Goodbye to the Valley

1949

Her name was Isha and she was the self-appointed flame-keeper for generations of the Tongva people who lived northwest of current day Los Angeles. The sound of bulldozers flattening oaks and orange orchards that surrounded her home inspired Isha to call me, her great grandniece and only living relative whose phone number she could find. At 90 years of age, Isha looked healthy enough and determined to hand down the history of our people.

When I arrived at her temporary motel, she was sitting on a neatly made bed, dressed and ready for me to take her to the top of Stoney Point. This iconic sentinel-like boulder formation has overlooked the San Fernando Valley for multi-millennia, and she thought it would be a good place to say goodbye to the region that meant so much to her. There was an urgency in her voice when she called and I understood that everything in the Valley was changing fast; one day here, the next day gone.

I worried she wouldn't be able to manage the narrow, winding trail to the top, how could I explain it if I let this tiny old lady topple off the Point. She assured me that she had been climbing up Stoney Point since she was a girl, so I reluctantly agreed to the plan. I would have been more enthusiastic, but the weather was so fine, and my children wanted to go to the beach.

I hadn't seen Isha for years and was surprised at how feisty and energetic the old girl was. I was relieved when we arrived at the top of Stoney Point with no need to run for help, but I had to draw the line when she wanted to carve *Isha Was Here* on the side of a boulder. She darted a defiant look at me that said, 'I will if I want to' and I could see her mind turning on a way to outwit me. I'd heard family stories that she'd been an independent kid who liked to do things her way and I studied her, wondering what she had up her sleeve.

She was right, I should know more about our shared family histories. Her ancestors were primarily valley Tongva and mine were mostly coastal Malibu Chumash—I pictured them in a black and white newsreel, but to Isha they were all colorfully alive in that active imagination of hers. I decided to be a good listener and make an old lady feel better by letting her share the knowledge with me.

We sat on the most comfortable rock we could find that overlooked the Valley and she began by gesturing to bulldozers close enough to hear their roar. This dramatic touch emphasized there was little time left to witness the remnants of our ancestral valley as we had known it in our lifetime.

On cue, the biggest bulldozer had a tree in its claw, gave a mighty jerk and with the grinding of gears and a roar that echoed into the valley, yanked the tree and tossed it aside. Oranges went flying. A few minutes before it was a living thing that had gone through the seasons on that spot, but it was now refuse.

It was theatrical, but Isha could not have picked a better moment to illustrate the clearing away of history. The point was not lost on me, but my mind was flitting about to other pressing things in my life and to the day I was missing at the beach. Terrible great grandniece that I was, I only paid half-attention to this earnest little old person.

Isha took on an air of dignified importance as she began to speak again. She certainly looked the part of an elder storyteller as she pulled herself upright, her snow-white hair was held tight in a bun and her centuries old Chumash beaded, abalone necklace glowed in April sunlight.

"Deep in the Valley," for added effect, she gestured again to the Valley below, "time flowed seamlessly for thousands of years."

I rolled my eyes and got another testy look from her.

"...for thousands of years, until strangers arrived and carved up the land. They put up fences and missions and ever since then there has been trouble with who owns what..."

Isha was interrupted by a thudding of horse hooves on the path below. Men's voices too.

"Now what?" She complained.

We waited a bit trying to figure out who in the world would bring a horse to the top, then a big movie camera appeared around the corner of a boulder, quickly followed by the photographer and a film crew. Then came a magnificent white stallion that took my breath away. It was fitted with bright, silver-studded reins and black studded saddle and then, if that wasn't enough, I could not believe my eyes, there was the Lone Ranger. Who else could it be with the horse Silver! He was wearing a broad smile and all the Lone Ranger regalia, including the hat, and his mask was peeking out of his white shirt pocket.

Isha didn't watch television, so this meant nothing to her, but later she did comment on what a lovely horse and handsome man that was. The crew edged past us, apologizing profusely as it was a tight squeeze. The Lone Ranger was charming, tipped his hat to us and said "Ladies" as he led Silver to the crew. They set up cameras and large reflectors, then filmed only 20 feet away for the iconic shot where, at the end of every episode thereafter, Silver reared high and the Lone Ranger declared "Hi-Yo Silver, and away!" I was thrilled by all this, but Isha was more confused than anything. When they offered me an extra's part in filming an episode the following week, I was too excited to hear the rest of Isha's boring tale.

The crew left, and I thought one of them winked at me. Isha was ready to begin again.

"Deep in the valley…, Nancy, are you listening?"

Isha, I can't do this now, there is too much happening. Let's drive to the orchard, I haven't seen it for years. Isha agreed; I could see she was tired, like she was holding up the weight of her 90 years and the burden of history. I began to feel her urgency.

On the way to the orchard, Isha regained enough strength to continue her message.

"Nancy, if you were a bird today flying over the Santa Suzanna hills, Stoney Point and Chatsworth, you would see an army of bulldozers chewing up the whole San Fernando Valley. In the not-too-distant past, open land was carved into smaller and smaller pieces, first the vast Ranchos, then large orchards were reduced to small orchards and now little yards for all the people moving to California."

I nodded, trying hard to listen, but when I pulled onto a strange two-lane paved road, I swiveled my head around.

"Wait", I said, "where are we? Did I take a wrong turn? Shouldn't we be in the middle of the orchard, not on a paved road? Look, there's the packing shed that was supposed to be deep in the orchard."

"You see what I'm saying?" She said.

I said, "Look at all the tract houses on the right, all done up with faux-ranch style trim and with each style repeated, it looks like every 5th house…I can tell where the repetition begins because it starts with a lime green color."

I drove another minute but was too confused to go further; I didn't trust my senses and pulled over to the side of the new road to settle down. Where we stopped was worse. The air was filled with engine noise and the diesel smell of the bulldozers flattening the land in preparation for new lime green houses. In the distance the sound of buzzsaws and hammering came from another building site.

I was about to start the engine when a wild-eyed, skinny horse bolted out of what was left of the orchard and across the street.

"That must be old Ferguson's horse," said Isha, "they haven't been able to find him since all the ruckus started."

In the distance, a motorcycle club rounded a corner that hadn't been there before and was approaching us from the opposite direction. The roar of 20 or so engines passing made Isha put her frail hands over her ears.

Isha said, "the strip of our orchard is so narrow now, you can see traffic on either side if you look right or left. I our family lived and worked at that orchard for most of my life and it was trees all the way to the hills."

The new road was disorienting with landmarks of my childhood visits gone. The sound of the motorcycle squadron reverberated in my head and only the faint, but intoxicating smell of citrus told me where we were. We got out of the car and looked at bruised oranges in Sunkist packing boxes that had been left, forgotten, on the packing shed porch.

Overhead a distant sputtering was coming closer. We

looked up to see a little plane dragging a large banner advertising *Grand Opening*, then the little plane continued East to the rest of the Valley.

"Isha, I'm exhausted, you must be too. Why don't we go back to my house in Reseda and call it a day. We can come back tomorrow, and you can finish your story."

"Our story."

For the first time that day I saw her smile, a big, glorious smile that showed her new dentures.

"You like my new teeth?" Her old woman's laugh sounded somewhere between a chuckle and a cackle. "There're some things that aren't so bad about the modern world."

The next day I told my office I had family matters to attend to and we hiked back up Stoney Point. It was probably the slowest hike on record, anything slower would have been like standing still, but we made it once again without incident. I couldn't help myself; I kept scouting the road below to see it a movie crew was coming, but there was no masked man in sight.

"Deep in the Valley...

Are you listening??

"Yes," I had been very careful not to roll my eyes.

Isha continued, "When my father was a boy, the Tongva hunted and dry-farmed right down there. She waved her arm to encompass the whole corner of the valley. There was little water then, before Water and Power did their thing. Every summer, they trekked across the hills through the Topanga canyon to Malibu and partied and traded with your Chumash people, our coastal cousins. Sometimes they took our father out to the islands to fish.

One day, on their return trip from the ocean, Spanish missionaries came to save them from this 'terrible way of life' and took them to the Mission San Fernando. Large ranchos had been granted, so instead of hunting and fishing, they were put to work on them. Then came the wars with Mexico and the Treaty of Hildago in 1848 and the land was carved up again and doled out to different people.

Some of the Mexican families were allowed to keep their property for a while and I knew Senora Vega, who owned the land where the orchard stands now. I was just a girl and babysat her grandchildren on the large veranda while she sat at the far end managing the rancho and tending to her caged birds. Sweet air came from the lush, citrus garden and she liked to tend the Bougainvillea and herbs that grew abundantly in the many glazed pots lining the garden. She was happy there, listening to her birds and greeting guests who arrived from surrounding ranchos, but eventually, she too had to leave.

Businessmen came to town and carved the land into even smaller pieces and turned this part of the valley into orange and walnut orchards. And now, you see, the bulldozers are scraping up the trees to carve the land into tinier pieces for people who want to be suburbanites with a swimming pool. I can't get over the swimming pools that are everywhere when I think of how my father had to farm with buckets of water from a little creek."

I said, "Where is all that water coming from?"

"I don't know, something about politics and a dam. Anyway, Nancy, I don't know what would become of me if it weren't for you, my brother's daughter's daughter, who has an apartment behind her house in Reseda."

I never imagined the visit would turn out the way it did. I thought I'd never see my great grandaunt again, but Isha continued to share stories with my family that were gathered from hundreds of years of history, and she restored a sense of kinship with the land, my ancestors and myself.

I asked one day why she never wore that pretty Chumash beaded and abalone shell necklace, she shrugged.

"Oh, I must have accidentally dropped it between the cracks of those boulders at Stoney Point."

So that was her plan. I remembered that feisty look she gave me when I told her she shouldn't carve her name on the rock at Stoney Point.

I said "Accidentally?"

"Uh huh…"

I had to smile. It was easy to picture her as the self-willed child that family stories reported little Isha to be, and I could imagine the imperious Sonora Vega's consternation when confronted with her incorrigible young babysitter.

Isha later fessed up and said she wanted to leave something for the valley to remember her by. Well, Isha, I thought, those rocks and your necklace will be there for thousands of years to come guarding the history of the valley of which you are so much a part.

House of Truth

1924

Movement caught my Grandmother Clara's eye while hiking from the beach up the Santa Monica bluff. High on the hill above the Pacific, sylph-like figures undulated gracefully in loose-fitting gowns on a Grecian-looking terrace.

Clara was a midwestern columnist who wrote gossipy, fluffy lifestyle pieces and was looking for stories in Los Angeles with a little more substance to them about modern life on the coast in the 1920s.

She pointed to the terrace and said to her friend Harry, a hardboiled LA Tribune reporter, "That looks like an interesting subject for a story, not something you see in Kansas."

"Funny you should mention that, I know the husband of the house, or should I say house-husband—he's a good friend of mine and I've been worried about him. I'll give him a call to see when he and his wife, the prima donna up there in the purple, would be available. He's married to Madame Selena, the House of Truth guru."

"Who?

"You haven't heard of Madame Selena? She has thrown together random bits of eastern religions and has made a semi-coherent mishmash of it all. She indoctrinates her followers as though she knows what she's talking about and claims she has a pipeline to the truth. She flies all around Southern California in her airplane that has the *House of Truth* painted on the sides and people have been known to move to LA to be close to her. She's drummed up a big following and a correspondingly big bank account."

Clara was all ears. There weren't many religions to choose from in Kansas and she thought her readers would like to see how Californians exercised their spirituality. She'd been researching the multitude of old religions in Los Angeles and now was eager to see what Madame Selena was all about—she was ready for something a little exotic to spice up her dispatches to the Midwest.

She had recently done a piece on the landscape architecture of Pershing Square, an improbably lush park that had no comparison to anything in Kansas. It was loaded with subtropical trees, movie stars and all kinds of people who rubbed elbows there due to its location at the intersection of the theater, civic and financial districts. It was a magnet for religious speakers, actors, theatergoers, financial barons and city officials.

Clara had just filed a series of well received articles reporting on what the Hollywood stars were up to and wanted to turn her attention to local politics, but backed off that subject after Harry told her, "Too dangerous, there are serious connections between organized crime and City Hall—otherwise known as the City Hall Gang."

Disappointed, she thought about what to do next. She continued to write pieces on the golden Southern California weather, sunbathers, muscle builders on the beach, and the curious oil wells that had sprouted all over the city landscape.

She also investigated for her readers in Kansas the amazingly diverse spiritual practices in town. Pershing Square had preachers of all persuasions, including the people who walked around with sandwich boards hanging from their shoulders warning 'The End Is Near' to speakers representing semi-established organizations like Aimee Simple McPhearson.

She researched the different churches she had driven past LA. Many were well-established, world-wide religions like Buddhists, Christian Scientists, Zoroastrianism, Confucianism, Hinduism, Sikhs, Sufis, Protestants, Catholics and Greek Orthodox. In the process, she attended Christian Science lectures where everyone sat politely in folding chairs and spent time studying in their comfortable Reading Rooms that were scattered throughout the city. She learned about the ancient mysteries of middle eastern Zoroaster and how to twirl like a Sufi to reach a transcendental state. She sang hymns in a Methodist church, heard the bells and inhaled the incense of Catholicism.

Those religions were established, at least in some part of the world, but she also wanted to learn more about the significant number of Angelinos who devoted their time and money to the far-flung spiritual fringes that were of the 'only in LA' variety. Clara knew this would boggle the collective mind of her practical, midwestern, newspaper readership.

These devotees often espoused allegiance to a particular local personality or sought connection to the primal being through sunbathing, mountain climbing or cave dwelling. LA in the 1920's was a perfect place where, if you wanted to start a religion honoring a moon goddess, divining meaning from tea leaves or the contours of the clouds passing overhead, there were people in LA ready to hand you cash to hear your words of wisdom.

Harry talked about his friend on the way to visit the house they had seen the week before.

"Walter's an attorney and lately he's been a stockbroker on the side. We went to school together. He's a bona fide genius and good guy. Knowing him, I think he's on the up and up, even though lately he's been selling oil stocks to some of the disreputable people who work at City Hall, you know, the 'City Hall Gang' I told you about. If it wasn't good old Harry, I would assume there was something shady going on. I must say, he's changed since he married Selena a couple of years ago, more reclusive and doesn't stay downtown to have a drink like he used to. Guess that's normal when you get married though."

Clara raised a reporter's suspicious eyebrow, "I thought oil investments in LA were risky since many of them are notoriously over-sold, in other words, worthless."

"Not good old Walter, he is as straight arrow as they come. I've known him for 29 years, solid as a rock. I never would have figured, though, he could be swept off his feet by a flamboyant diva-type like his new wife. Wait until you meet him, he is so button-down, he looks like he'd fit into your Kansas crowd. She's got a grip on Walter and his money, and she's squeezing him hard. What can you do, the poor man is smitten."

There was no place left to park in front of the big, pink colonnaded house, so Harry parked the Roadster down the hill and looked up at the colorful home of button-down Walter, a lawyer wo Harry described as never leaving never leaving the house without a hat, tie and neutral three-piece suit. The house clearly reflected the style of his eccentric bride.

"Look up there," Harry pointed, "Selena is the leader in the saffron and purple robe. She must be teaching them her hodgepodge of philosophies—she espouses the ancient Egyptian sun god who is all powerful, Indian chakras that orients the center of your being around your spine, and how to connect through movement with the divine spirits of the sun, wind, water, and earth. Then later today, she will put them to work and send them out into the neighborhoods of Los Angeles, each with an offering jar to spread the word about the House of Truth."

Clara said, "You know, I think I could be easily swayed by someone who could teach me how to relax. I'm intrigued by the Indian Chakra thing, and I like to meditate. Giving thanks to the sun, sand and sea is not a bad idea. It's the thought of giving a lot of money to Selena that tenses me up."

"Yes, and she'd love your money, believe me, their lifestyle doesn't come cheap. They do their water ablutions and sunbathing all around the world. And of course, fine wine and food are all part of nature so they should indulge in the best and most expensive. A City attorney doesn't make that much money."

"I thought he was a stockbroker too," Clara said.

"True, but he's only been selling oil stocks lately in his spare time, I guess to give the proceeds to Selena. I tell you— he's hooked. Oil stocks are a gamble, there's so much cheating going on, but there's money to be made in oil investment, even for an honest oil stock salesman who doesn't sell overissued stock. Walter might look ordinary, but he's brilliant and has been able to figure out where the gushers flow and only sells stock in the ones in which he believes."

"That's a handy skill to have."

"Indeed."

Clara overcame her aversion to the pink color and was impressed when they walked up in front of the big house with Grecian columns lining the large porch. A beige-looking man answered the door. Sandy-blonde hair, tan gaberdine suit, and even beige socks; only the horn-rimmed glasses and a lawyerly self-assurance stood out on him.

"Hello, Walter."

"Harry, old friend, I've been hoping to see you!" His enthusiastic greeting revealed a buoyant personality that belied that washed-out first impression and his animated features made him handsome. He slapped Harry on the back and pumped my hand in greeting.

"It was great to hear from you, it's been a while, I don't get out much these days, please come in! I was just making a cocktail—would you like one? It's my own creation—vermouth, vodka, and a brandy float."

Although it wasn't lunchtime yet, we accepted a drink to be sociable. Walter led us to the back of the house and stopped at the bar by the glass doors facing the balcony and ocean.

Harry turned to me and pointed to the dozens of red roses in a large crystal vase.

"Walter is a well-trained husband—he stops at the flower stall by Pershing Square once or twice week and buys Selena flowers." Harry waved his hand to indicate a living room filled with a variety of flowers on every tabletop.

Clara smiled at Walter and said, "Selena is a lucky woman to get all that attention, they are lovely."

Walter started topping off the cocktails with the brandy float when Harry put on his reporter's voice as a warning to his friend and queried, "I heard a rumor that flower stall is being used by foreign investments to funnel money into a laundering scheme. Of course, customers wouldn't suspect anything like that from a little wooden shack of a flower stall."

Clara had been listening with one ear and watching Selena leading the group at the same time. She got the drift that Harry was pushing an agenda and exclaimed good-naturedly, "You reporters, always looking for a story." Harry got the message and smiled at Walter. They clinked glasses and toasted, "To all our years of friendship."

Through the window, Clara's attention was drawn back to Selena as her diaphanous gown swirled and jewel-like decorations flashed on her headband.

"Golly," she said, "that's quite a woman."

She shook her curly blond head and tried to imagine her folksy self trying to carry off that look, especially while leading a group of goddess-like creatures through sophisticated free-form moves borrowed from modern and East Indian dance.

We didn't go out on the deck until Madame Selena clapped her hands and the fluid, expressionistic moves stopped instantly. We didn't want to interrupt but misjudged the clapping cue, she wasn't ready for us yet, so the three of us sat under the shade of a eucalyptus tree at the end of the deck.

Selena's voice was entrancing as she led them in a breathing meditation, inhaling the ocean air and the scent of eucalyptus that covered much of the hillside, appreciating the sun on their shoulders, hearing the rustle of leaves, birds in the trees, and the waves that were close enough to sense their rhythm if not exactly hear them.

She intoned in a rich, seductive voice, "Feel the elements, they are the supreme being speaking to you and movement is your response. It is time to close, but remember, all the elements are in conversation with you."

Harry had to tap her shoulder to rouse Clara to the here and now. When they first arrived, she was anxious to get the whole thing over with, but Selena's voice had woven its spell and she hadn't felt so loose for years. Harry could see the effect Selena had on her and he kidded, "You warned me you were an easy target since you liked to think about your chakras, or something like that."

A few of the women remained on the deck to practice Sufi twirling to enhance spirituality, while others drifted inside and lolled on the plush couches with their yam cakes and tea that suspiciously put a glow on their cheeks and a faraway look in their eyes. Selena greeted us formally on the deck and did not look pleased to see Harry with Walter. Was there furtiveness in her glance? Did she not appreciate reporters in her house? Her speech had turned clipped and business-like; gone were the sonorous intonations, the entrancing words, and Clara could feel tension seeping back into her mind at the imperious, dismissive tone.

It was time to go. Madame Selena had left the deck and while Walter and Harry caught up on the old days, Clara took a deep breath and looked around. The light flowed in radiant streams through the clear, leaded balcony windows and she could feel some of the good energy return while bathed in this heavenly atmosphere. For a few moments she forgot about Selena's snippy tone, but she snapped back to earth when she spied the donation plate on the dining room table brimming with money in big denominations.

The last vestiges of Selena's hypnotic voice dropped away, the radiant light disappeared behind a mental cloud, and she felt manipulated. As they were leaving, she sensed that Walter was steering them as close as possible to the donation plate without being too obvious, but she edged Harry, perhaps a little more obviously, in the other direction and out the door.

Clara received a letter from Harry two weeks after returning to the conservative bastion of Kansas with colorful stories about wild and crazy Californians. Kansans loved to read about the goings-on in California so they could shake their heads and go "Tut-Tut" in disapproval.

But Madame Selena and Walter's story had taken a more bizarre turn that could have gotten her readers all going Tut-Tut-Tut-TutTut. She would never tell the tale in print— she wouldn't betray dear Harry's confidence and didn't think readers would even believe it if she did. Selena had been acting erratically, one minute singing and dancing like she didn't have a care in the world, and the next minute acting nervous. One night Walter found her frantically packing suitcases. Her voice took on a soothing tone that one might use to calm a child when she told them that they should take a little trip to Mexico after the LaMonica Ballroom grand opening on the Santa Monica pier that Saturday night.

'Trust me, darling, I must stay for the opening of the Ballroom. I'm on the organizing committee. We can take off that evening in my plane; it's been a long time since we have been to Mexico. Trust me, Darling'.

Walter called Harry to see if he could guess what Selena was up to and Harry tried without luck to use his reporter connections to learn what was going down. Walter told Harry that it was important to her to be at the big bash at the pier for the grand opening and they would meet at the airport to take off at midnight.

It was getting dark when Harry called Walter to warn him

that the authorities were coming that evening to raid their house looking for double books regarding the sale of oil stocks to city hall. Walter rushed to the pier, but five thousand people were attending the opening of the LaMonica and he abandoned his car in a monumental traffic jam at the waterfront. He ran down the pier and looked frantically for Selena in the packed ballroom. Wedged in the middle of the swaying crowd, he was bumping into people, trying to search over shoulders and even elbowing dancers out of the way.

Harry too had been caught in the mass of bodies until he finally saw his usually composed friend searching for Selena.

"Walter," he shouted, "she's gone, probably for the airport." Walter looked stricken and almost lost his footing in the crowd.

"She's gone?"

Harry had a Press Pass and was able to park his Roadster close to the ballroom—they arrived at the Butterfield-Santa Monica Airport in time to see the little House of Truth airplane picking up speed past the runway lights and veer west to soar over the night-black Pacific with ill-gotten gains and Walter's heart.

The Perfect Husband

Prologue

1924 Sheriff Bill's Announcement

The bells clanged on the Phoenix Rock and Fossil shop door when Sheriff Bill walked in with his usual bag of donuts. I had to admire how the blue uniform and the cap he wore at an angle made my old friend look imposing—not at all like the clutsy boy I knew in school. This morning though, his expression was unusually serious, and he dropped the bag with a thud by the coffee percolator and announced,

"Donuts!"

I put down the fossil I was labeling and said, "Good morning, Bill, I've never heard anyone say 'donuts' that way.

Bill cleared his throat, "I just got word from the Los Angeles Sheriff's Department—Jasper is at St Vincent's hospital—he's okay, more or less, he just can't remember the past year, luckily he had his ID on him."

Time stopped with the shock of Sheriff Bill's announcement and I was pulled back to a conversation with Jasper when we were young, before his obsession with elusive quests turned our lives upside down.

PART I

1911 The Quest

"*Stick with me, Flora, we're going to hit the jackpot.*"

"*How's that again?*"

"*I've got plans, one of them will hit it big and we'll be rolling in dough. I won't need my mother's money with all her strings attached. I want to buy you pretty things on my own.*"

"*I thought you wanted to make the world a better place.*"

"*That too, of course.*"

"*Let's get married and help me spend it.*"

"*And make the world a better place, right?*"

"*Of course. I've been thinking about the automobile—it will be a revolutionary democratizer of the world. A bank president will drive down the street bumper to bumper with the local grocer and they have to stop at the same signals.*"

"*You're such a dreamer.*"

"*An inventor must be a dreamer.*"

"*How is a grocer going to afford an automobile?*"

"*Believe me, they will, and this is where my idea comes in. It's an opportunity for me to invent new ways to turn sources of oil into affordable fuel for Model Ts, the mass-produced automobile for grocers and all the average people.*"

"*But they are already creating chaos in downtown Phoenix, it's not safe to bring my horse down there anymore.*"

"*Horses are out, automobiles are in, and people are on the move. It's the same everywhere, from Los Angeles to New York City, and these inventions I've been thinking about will help keep democracy humming.*"

~~~~~~~~~~

I often mused on this long-ago conversation while waiting for Jasper to return from his many subsequent quests, each one a little less idealistic than the last. We met at the University of Arizona when Jasper was a charming boy with a head full of high-minded ideas about how to use his new mineralogy diploma. I was more down to earth...literally...plugging along on my geology degree and, despite my bad vision, studying rocks and fossils through a microscope.

He said I would fit right into the family—his father was a down-to-earth geologist and that's why he named his only son Jasper after one of his favorite rocks. He didn't mention that his mother had no resemblance to this image he painted of his family, she was completely stuck on herself as a New York City society maven. I couldn't imagine how Jasper's father and mother ever got together, but she never left New York these days, so out of sight, out of mind. We were married the same day we celebrated the opening of Flora's Rock and Fossil shop in Phoenix and his mother only sent a card.

Opening the Rock and Fossil shop gave me a chance to share the surprising things one could find underfoot in the Arizona desert. Brilliant gems lay hidden in the dusty, monotone landscape, and evolutionary stories were waiting to be told by fossils like Pleistocene fish swimming in a sea of desert sand. Jasper's interest in what lay hidden in the desert was more utilitarian. Oil, silver and gold, that's what he looked for, not for their innate characteristics, but what could be created with them. Oil in particular was going to transform society, and he wanted to be part of this democratic revolution by inventing ways to extract it and use it. I was mesmerized by handsome Jaspers's cleverness and talk of high-minded pursuits.

I sometimes wondered what he saw in me. He said he admired my mind, but when people say that it's not always a compliment. Jasper was popular and thriving in the moment, while I was stuck in prehistory and living a quiet life talking to fossils. When I wasn't investigating past epochs through a microscope, I had my nose in a book by ancient authors. He patted me on the head and said, "Flora. pretty gems and fossil collecting are important too." He had said this to be kind, however, my work did sound paltry and irrelevant compared to his quest to improve the nation's transportation system for the benefit of mankind and get rich at the same time.

But high-mindedness coupled with ambition and a lack of money can be a slippery thing to hold onto and Jasper's quest had proved elusive. There was so much competition in this new age and other inventors with more resources beat him to the punch, sometimes by a matter of a few months. I pretended not to notice him unraveling a bit after each setback. Jasper always needed to be in pursuit of something new and meaningful, but things were not going his way. He was confused and embarrassed, so I concentrated on my work and averted my attention to the minutiae I could see through the microscope on my desk; the mysteries of the crystalline structures of rocks and deciphering the story of a fossil were less confusing than knowing how to help Jasper find his bearings.

1923 The Quest Grinds On

I was watching Jasper navigate his vulnerable-looking Model T around an expanse of Mesquite in the Arizona desert. He was off to Los Angeles again to promote his latest invention with investors and had gotten a late start. The sun was high—really beating down now—and the heat was steaming up my new spectacles. I wiped them and put them back on, but they were too big and slipped down my nose. I took off my straw hat to fan my face, but quickly put it back on again to keep the sun out of my eyes. The hat didn't block enough of the glare—the brightness found its way under the brim and up from the desert floor. It also couldn't keep my thick brown hair from falling out of my bun and blanketing my shoulders.

I pulled my hair up and secured it back under the hat. What a relief with the weight off my shoulders. A refreshing little breeze blew across my neck and gave a momentary respite from the heat, but this was quickly replaced by a stab of guilt when I realized I had compared my beautiful Jasper to a weight on my shoulders. But there was no denying it, I was relieved to see his silhouette fading into the distance.

I wiped away a trickle of sweat close to my eye and thought about what a complainer the middle-aged Jasper had become. The other day he said, "Your bun makes you look old-fashioned, like a pre-war schoolteacher." This confused me because he had always said my hair was lovely and that he liked taking it down at night. All in one breath, he carried on, "While you're bringing yourself into the 20th century, you could ditch those clunky new glasses for something sexier...and one more thing, when you part your hair in the middle, it makes you look like a schoolteacher...no, more like the school principal." I tried to not take his complaints to heart but considered getting rimless glasses and bobbing my hair.

His inventions were not selling, and Jasper went into a tailspin. His birthday was coming up and making him feel the pinch of time.

He was only turning 37 but he thought of himself as middle-aged now. He complained that he didn't know how many dreams he had left, and that he lost a piece of himself each time he shoved the plans for unsold machinery to the back of a shelf along with an ever-growing collection of others. Every time he looked at this shelf of broken dreams, his ambitions turned a little stiff and bleaker.

One afternoon, I was stunned to find him ripping his beautiful technical drawings, the manifestations of his dreams, off the sitting room wall. In my mind, they were art and an insight into his far-flung imagination. Protesting, I followed him out to the backyard of our little adobe ranch house where he jammed them into the incinerator and, in the turbulence of an oncoming monsoon, he tried to light a bonfire.

When a few big drops of rain landed he yelled at the darkening skies, but his complaint was swept away in the wind. He hurled the entire box of matches into the flames and laughed as an ineffective burst left a soggy mess of paper. A huge lightning bolt streaked through the dark clouds and a long roll of thunder vibrated the ground—the monsoon had begun in earnest. I'd never seen Jasper in such turmoil. His face was filled with shame and anger as I hurried him into our little home to get out of the sudden downpour, and that night I could only commiserate with him.

Imagine my surprise when he breezed into the kitchen the next morning enthused with a new idea—investing in oil would make us rich and that would fund his new ideas for inventions.

"It will be simple—all I have to do is buy stocks in the booming Los Angeles oil market or lease a plot of land near one of that area's many promising wells."

To my shock, he threw just a few things into a suitcase and off he went that morning to Los Angeles. Again.

He returned a week later flush with money but with only a convoluted explanation. I realized soon that his reasons were incoherent because he wanted to avoid telling me that his well-to-do mother, who had been thousands of miles away most of his life, agreed to loan him the money.

"How did you talk her into that?"

"I convinced her of what a great investment it is for her too and I also laid on a heavy dose of guilt. She owes me."

I wanted to rage at her for hurting my Jasper with her selfish disregard, but instead I would have to show gratitude for a bail-out. Worse than this, however, was the tremulous excitement in Jasper's voice, and the terrible gleam in his eyes that made me shiver.

That evening, I started a letter to her, not with a word of thanks for something I didn't request, but with a suggestion that Jasper was acting a little manic these days. I tore it up. How was I going to tell that woman I thought her son was going over the edge with his obsessive quests, especially since her own husband was lost in a snowstorm in the Yukon while determined to find gold. Was Jasper, like his father, off on a fool's errand? I wished I had paid more attention to what was happening lately instead of looking through my microscope, and when I tried to connect the dots, I couldn't.

~~~~~~~~~~

I was wilting in the heat and could only imagine how hot Jasper would be on his trip—I wanted to protect him and called out to him to please come back, but he was too far away. The sound of clamoring and pounding from a little copper mining town wafted down from a far-away hilltop as I watched the spindly tires of the Model T convertible swerving around an occasional Mesquite bush or perhaps a rattlesnake. Jasper's quest this time was to check on the reported oil sands further north before turning west to Los Angeles. I shaded my eyes as I watched the little convertible head deeper into the unknown. He turned and waved, but I wasn't quick enough for him to see me wave back, and I could only watch the car bounce along until all I could make out was the outline of his fedora and shoulders as the skinny wheels kicked up dust.

My eyes ached from straining after him, so I focused on things nearby to give them a break. Not too far away was an interesting-looking rock that must have been dislodged from a mound by a recent monsoon and its rough edges stood out clearly in the smooth-grained sand. I picked it up, blew away the ancient dust, and exposed a tiny fish fossil, maybe a Cyprinodon Macularus. "Hello little fellow." I said, "What are you doing out here all by yourself, have you been waiting millennia for me to find you?"

I carried the prize over to my Model T truck and put it on the passenger seat. "We're heading back to my rock and fossil shop where you can join other fossils about your age." I enjoyed making friends with my fossils, but this habit annoyed Jasper to no end so I didn't chatter on.

Maybe it was the sun beating down on my head, but when I climbed behind my steering wheel, I had a long-avoided vision. I saw Jasper on a never-ending quest and our lives forever topsy-turvy, dominated by this continual striving for a pot of oil or money behind a phantasmal rainbow.

The gulf between us had never been as wide. We were like an evolving species headed in different directions. While Jasper was out trekking all over the West looking for that rainbow, I'd settled into a peaceful, if somewhat humdrum existence of running my shop by day, and at night, reading at my Victorian desk in my room on the second floor. I had stopped going to our adobe when he was gone, there were too many memories there.

I sat in my little truck trying to cool down with a Japanese fan Jasper had brought back from a convention in San Francisco. It was too hot to think anymore—thank goodness, no more thinking! I took a handkerchief from my skirt pocket to wipe away beads of perspiration before I realized they were tears. To settle my mind, I thought about which books in the shop's library might have information about the little fish forever swimming in the big rock on the seat where Jasper used to sit. I pulled the starter and as the engine made encouraging noises, I took one last look at the horizon. Jasper had completely vanished in little puffs of desert sand and that last obscure image stayed with me for a full year.

~~~~~~~~~~

1924 One Year Later

It was another hot Arizona morning, and a blue-blue sky lit the long shop windows, the thermometer outside read 95 degrees, and a table fan was losing its battle with the rising heat. A coffee percolator smelled inviting, and the wall clock said it was almost time for the Rock and Fossil shop to open. All was still.

Anne, a young Native American woman in a beaded, robin's-egg blue tunic was sitting at a worktable surrounded by semiprecious stones and jewelry-making paraphernalia. The clock ticked to 9:00, and she automatically stood up, unlocked the shop door, and turned the open sign around.

Quiet mornings like this prepared me to meet the day— only the sound of a chattering Cactus wren in the saguaro outside, the rustle of turning pages of the Fish Fossils of the

Southwest book, and Anne arranging semiprecious stones into a necklace could be heard. I walked around for a minute to survey the shop. Everything was in order, neatly labeled and dusted. Peaceful—until I accidentally looked in the direction of the front door where there hung a large missing person poster with a picture of a smiling Jasper. I averted my eyes quickly to avoid feeling sick.

I sat back down to continue reading about the fish fossil, but after a minute the clanging bells over the shop door announced a tourist who wanted to see Anne about a necklace he ordered for his wife. The necklace was ready, and the man left exceedingly pleased.

I thought he'd never leave; I had no patience for people since Jasper had been gone. I was more nervous every day and the only thing that got my mind off wondering what happened to him was delving into research. I considered opening the shop at noon and taking those bells down, they were too annoying. Anne said I was getting more skittish than a scaredy cat and that little interruptions were annoying me—even paying customers.

Ever since my revelation the day I watched Jasper disappear into the desert I pledged to pay more attention to what was happening around me, to not be lost in my microscope and books. Could Jasper's disappearance have been prevented if I had been a better wife and stopped hiding from the situation behind my microscope before he disappeared into that dust cloud in the desert. When it became clear he was missing a year ago, I pledged I would stop merely hoping for the best and would always be vigilant. It was exhausting. Anne was right, I was like a nervous cat.

PART II

Sheriff Bills explanation about Jasper as told by Anne:

"Flora, you had gone back to reading about fossils, but Sheriff Bill opened the door with such force that the bells clanged even louder this time, and you almost jumped out of your chair. You muttered something under your breath about those darn bells and I agreed with what I thought you probably said that we needed to get something that sounded more musical for the door.

Sheriff Bill blustered in with his usual bag of donuts.

I was concentrating on my work but something about Bill's entrance made me apprehensive and I looked up from the jewelry table.

"What's up, Bill?" I said.

Sheriff Bill's look turned from stern to confused. He almost threw down the bag of donuts, hemmed and hawed for a minute, then put on the official face again and told us about Jasper being in Los Angeles and how he was found not far from Durango, Mexico, stumbling out of the Sierra Madre mountains by himself. Bill said that Jasper was in bad shape, he was probably beaten by claim jumpers—he revived fairly well after a few days in the hospital but had no memory of the past year.

I said, "What, he has amnesia? I didn't think that was a real thing!"

I looked at you to see your reaction, but you must have been in shock. You were just staring at Bill like you didn't know who he was. Finally, you came to and said 'What'?

Bill continued with the news, "Apparently amnesia is a real thing. He had identification and remembered Phoenix and Flora, but he doesn't know what happened to his car, or how he got to Mexico. It looked like he had been in the part of the mountains where there had been recent gold claims, and they figure he had by been attacked by claim-jumpers and was hit hard on the head."

I wanted to take the train that afternoon to Los Angeles, but the tracks had been washed out by last week's monsoon and were still being repaired. Bill suggested I fly with Old Roy who owned the Lazy T Ranch.

Í said, "Isn't old Roy about a hundred by now? He was old when I was a kid."

"No. he claims to be still in his 70's, he just looks older from being out on the ranch all the time. He flies to Los Angeles and all over for business meetings—these days, he's more of a wheeling and dealing businessman than a rancher. He's flying to Santa Monica tomorrow morning—he flies there many times a year and he can take you to the little airport there. You could get a cab into downtown Los Angeles."

I'd never flown before, I didn't even like looking out a second story window. I was wondering how to talk Bill into turning around on the way to the airstrip. When we got there, I looked at the old plane with one engine and four wings and an old man in the cockpit and I wouldn't get out of the patrol car. Bill put his arm around my shoulder and used a low, soothing voice,

"Come on now, Flora, don't be afraid, herding cattle in the desert makes Roy look older than he is—probably closer to his 60s than his 80s, and he keeps his plane in tip-top shape."

It didn't look in tip-top shape to me with rusty looking bolts holding some dented pieces together. Bill picked up my suitcase and ushered me to the rickety-looking plane.

I stalled for time, "Stop a second, I want to smell the mesquite in the air." I got a whiff of the plane's exhaust instead of mesquite and coughed. "That's enough air." Weakened by a coughing fit, I allowed myself to be led up to the plane with Roy's Flying Bar X ranch brand painted on the side. The brave face I tried to put on must have turned into shock when Roy turned around and I got a close-up of his sun-withered face. If I wasn't being gently prodded by Bill I might have been walking backwards.

"He's left his 70s behind a while ago." I told Bill.

"He's not as old as he looks," Bill reiterated, as if saying it made it true.

With an extra shove from Bill, I got a few steps closer to the noisy plane. The wind from the engine blew my hair every which way, my bun came loose, and I could see my hair flying around. Roy was wearing a fringed leather jacket and cowboy scarf around his neck, all at odds with his goggles and aviator hat. His face developed even more wrinkles when he smiled encouragingly and motioned for me to climb aboard.

"Morn'n Ma'am, I hear you're goin' to Tinseltown. I'm jussay'n, be careful. Been meanin' to check out your old fossils I've heard about in your store but been busy with city folk stayin' at the ranch. Don't you worry now," he patted the cockpit for effect, "I fly Betsy here regularly to business meetin's and such. See more of Betsy these days than I do my cows."

I thought about making a run for it across the desert straight back to Phoenix, but Bill was standing in my way. It was no use protesting and soon I was in my seat behind old Roy.

"You'll be there by this afternoon, good luck in Los

Angeles," said Bill. I tried to smile back, but my face wouldn't move.

Roy handed me an aviator hat and goggles. "Hope that hat fits over all that lovely hair. Just to keep you busy, you can be my navigator by looking down and let'n me know when you see the concrete arrows on the ground that point the way to California." Roy looked at my petrified face and added "Just kid'n".

"What?" I could barely hear him over the sound of the engine getting louder. Something about needing my help finding Los Angeles. I looked at Bill in astonishment that I was about to go up in the air, then clenched my eyes as Roy started taxiing Betsy down the runway. I opened them hesitantly when Roy punched the engine and we took off sharply into the clear desert sky.

I looked back and down over the edge of the plane with my stomach in my throat and I could see the straight concrete strip of runway that looked out of place in the middle of the scattered brush and open desert. The little strip got smaller and smaller before I clenched my eyes again and wrung my hands all the way to Santa Monica. Closing my eyes might not have been the best idea as the blankness allowed me to visualize the jagged mountains that separate Los Angeles from the rest of the world. I concentrated on mentally willing old Roy to navigate the mountain pass by Palm Springs through which he'd have to thread the plane. While I was at it, I also willed the weather to be clear with no obscuring LA fog and the engine to not conk out.

I ignored the cabdriver's look of amusement. "I see people come out of that airport in all different states, but lady, you take the cake." I probably looked exactly the way I felt.

"Please, just take me to St Vincent's Hospital downtown."

I was excited to see Jasper again, but it didn't seem real. I'd begun to think I'd ever see him again and didn't know what to expect, but my misgivings melted away when I saw him. He had a permanent limp, but didn't know how it happened. He looked thin, bruised and tired, like he had been through a lot in the past year, but when we hugged, the old emotion between us was still there.

It was good that he remembered me and things that pertained to our past, but he didn't remember everything. He was different somehow. I asked what he wanted to do next, and he had no plans.

"What? Jasper with no plans?" He always had several plans that he had to start immediately.

"Nothing comes to mind. I'm looking forward to getting home to our little ranchette, maybe getting a horse or two and a dog."

"You'd have to stay home a lot to take care of them, I'm at the Rock and Fossil shop during most days."

"I have nowhere I want to go; I'd like to help at the shop and learn to cook. Maybe meet up with the guys at the coffee shop in the mornings."

He kept smiling and hugging me. "It's just so strange, not knowing I had gone so far away or even why. A year of my life, gone. I'm sticking around town from now on."

The last thing he remembered was driving across the desert to Los Angeles. I explained we had authorities looking for him an entire year, but that part of Mexico was not really in our search area.

I hoped that his memory of the past year wouldn't return, it must have been terrible. I wondered what would happen to his bucolic vision of life once he got a horse or two and a dog if he suddenly remembered his elusive quests and started striving for things again; I worried he was getting too old to suffer much more disappointment.

We waited until the tracks were repaired and took the train home. On the way, he reminisced about his boyhood in Phoenix and going to school with me and Sheriff Bill. He remembered the people that were part of the neighborhood, including the mailman, his old buddy from high school who worked at the hardware store, and all the guys at the coffee shop. He said he had a lot of catching up to do.

Before he left, he had no time to hang out with anyone, there was always too much on his mind, too many things on his agenda given that one quest replaced another with increasing rapidity. There was always somewhere to go to, something to do, and relaxation was time wasted—he'd often say, "we're burning daylight".

He'd been watching the scenery go by when he said he'd like to polish rocks for Anne.

"Seriously?"

"Yes, I think rock polishing would be relaxing."

I said that was a wonderful idea but was thinking that I hadn't heard him using the words relaxing and fun for years, especially not in the same sentence. Sheriff Bill's never going to believe this, he used to say I needed someone more fun in my life—however, I think there might have been a touch of jealousy in that appraisal.

Jasper also forgot that he didn't have time or inclination to cook, but now he left the shop in the afternoon to pick up fresh items for dinner and cook gourmet meals. Mornings were devoted to socializing with the guys at the coffee shop and post office. They were happy and as surprised as I was.

Anne said, "How can one woman be so lucky, you have the perfect husband."

I just nodded and raised my shoulders in wonder.

That was before the most amazing thing happened. While waiting for a sauce to thicken or a stew to cook, Jasper developed the habit of wandering into the old workshop where his inventions lined the shelves like museum pieces. He'd fiddle around with a few things, more as a way of avoiding watching a pot start to boil.

One afternoon, he had a brain wave that he credits to the bump on his head—he put together a few pieces that were laying around on the bench for years and it occurred to him that it would be a perfect widget to fit into an assembly for a machine he had just heard about at the coffee shop. We became rich beyond imagination and Jasper spent more time on philanthropic duties than rock polishing, but he still had dinner on the table.

Printed in the United States
by Baker & Taylor Publisher Services